FAE BLOOD LINES

JESSICA BOLD

CHAPTER ONE

RUBY

The brutally cold wind and drizzle whipped across my face, sending shivers through my body as I fumbled in my bag to find my door key. My embroidered work polo stuck uncomfortably to my skin. Swearing under my breath, I finally grasped the key and took several shaky-handed attempts to unlock the door to my house. As I entered, I released a big sigh of relief to be in the warmth and comfort, particularly after a stressful day at work. Today would have been fine if It hadn't been for the other waitress; Dicky Vicky as I liked to call her. Vicky had an extreme superiority complex that made my blood boil, and her marriage issues were often the cause of the snide comments she routinely unleashed on me. Despite my having been at The Rose restaurant for longer than Vicky, she knew how to kiss arse and still felt that she held a senior position. Rob, the owner, was fully aware of Vicky's attitude problems, but based on what I had unfortunately witnessed from arriving early to work one morning, I knew exactly why he allowed her to continue her reign of terror. Despite Dicky Vicky, I actually had a fondness for working at The Rose, and Rob was a good boss overall. Looking down at the mashed potato remnants on my uniform, I could only huff at the lack of glamour in my life. Twenty-five years old and I had reverted to the days of wearing food. I began heading to the kitchen when I jumped at the sound of a stray cat screeching and then leaping in through the open window in the living room.

'What the hell?'

I shouted, heart pounding at the surprise commotion. The cat began running across the living room, bloodied paw prints marking the carpet, and then paused to stare me in the eyes. I noticed its leg was held up and there were patches of pure black fur missing, it looked awful. I put on my sweetest voice.

'Hey there kitty, I'm not going to hurt you.'

I kept my voice relatively quiet as I moved slowly towards it. The cat sat down, looking at me almost curiously, as though deciding whether to trust me or not. It allowed me to approach and gently stroke its head. Upon closer inspection, I became concerned that the leg could be broken, and based on the facial swelling, it may have attained a head injury. This cat needed a vet.

'Seriously?'

I moaned under my breath. The cat mewed at me, as if in agreement. Deciding I couldn't ignore this animal's suffering, I did the only thing I could, I searched the internet for a vet's number and rang it. The out-of-hours receptionist had a bored-sounding voice, as though I was disturbing her evening, and reluctantly made an appointment for me. After the phone call, I glanced at the cat who had made her way onto my rug to get comfortable.

'Great, thanks! Blood all over the rug!'

The cat mewed what I interpreted in my head as an apology. I ran upstairs and fumbled for some form of container to put the cat into, and settled on a cardboard box. The cat eyed me as I approached, tail swishing unhappily.

Please don't bite me.

Don't give me a reason to then.

I stopped dead as the voice sounded in my head. I hesitated for a moment, assessing the strange feline, before deciding my exhaustion was making my head mess with me, and continued to put the cat into the box. To my surprise it remained in the box, glaring at me.

When we arrived at the vets I could easily tell that the lady at the desk was the one who I had spoken to on the phone. Her face remained disinterested as she checked us in. She was a young girl, with bright purple hair, and It was clear that this was her student summer break job. She had no interest In the job, or providing an acceptable service. We occasionally had students at The Rose, and I hated every minute spent with the arrogant teenagers who had no concept of the real world.

After a good thirty-minute wait, and the cat not taking its large yellow disc eyes off me, we got called into the vet's room. The vet introduced herself as Sarah, and to both of our surprise, the cat jumped awkwardly from the box and laid itself on the examination table. It allowed Sarah to do a check over, and merely grumbled in discomfort as she checked what appeared to be the broken leg.

'She will need pain relief and X-rays for the leg. The blood seems to be from some scrapes and scratches that have stopped bleeding now.'

I was about to nod in agreement but quickly realised that this cat was going to cost me money. A cat that wasn't mine.

'I did explain to your receptionist that she isn't actually mine.'

Sarah nodded, her face suggesting that she didn't believe me, but she hovered a scanner over her anyway.

'Well she's not microchipped, so we can take her for 7 days and hope an owner comes forward.'

An uncomfortable knotting formed in my stomach at her words.

'What happens if no one comes forward in 7 days?'

Sarah shifted awkwardly before answering.

'It's likely she will be put to sleep.'

The words echoed in my mind, and I glanced down at the cat, who apparently was female. Her eyes penetrated through me, as though she were trying to communicate, begging me not to leave her here. I had previously contemplated getting a pet but had decided I didn't have the time for one. But now, with this helpless creature in front of me, I couldn't stop the words coming from my mouth.

'I could take her home.'

Sarah's face flashed shock, as though she had expected me to dump the cat and run.

'If that's allowed?'

Sarah nodded and offered that they would advertise the found cat for 7 days. She then went through a rundown of costs. The £600 estimate had my heart pounding, and my breath hitching. Thank goodness I had a credit card. The cat was taken from me, and I was ushered into the waiting room again to wait for my newly acquired pet to be x-rayed.

Around two hours later, the cat was brought back out to me, her front left leg covered in a large purple bandage that looked too big for her to manoeuvre. Sarah's face was a light smile as she explained that it was a fracture that would heal with rest. A sigh of relief escaped my lips, and despite the drug-fuelled look on the cat's face, she seemed relieved too. Paying the bill was painful, but I managed a tight smile at the disinterested receptionist.

'Right stray, here's a blanket for you to sleep on tonight, do me a favour and just do what the vet ordered.'

The cat tilted her head at me.

'You're lucky it was my window you jumped in, you chose the biggest sap you could find that's for sure! And we had better give you a name, stray seems too derogatory. How about Saffie?'

The cat let out a mew before a loud purr, and I took that to mean that she liked the name. Throughout the night I woke to check on her, and each time she simply stared me in the eyes as if trying to work me out. Finally, my alarm sounded and I had to get up for work despite being completely exhausted. Thankfully it was Vicky's day off and so It was just me, Rob, Gary the Chef, and the barmaid Annie. We worked through the relatively quiet lunch crowd without too much stress, and I was fortunate to be allowed to leave early. I was getting my coat on when Rob awkwardly approached me.

'Are you okay Ruby? You seem tired and distracted today.'

Rob commented, a concerned frown formed.

'I'm okay, just tired. I kind of adopted a broken cat.'

I lightly chuckled, but his confused face encouraged me to elaborate.

'A stray found her way to my house with a broken leg, and me being the mug I am, I've taken her in.'

Rob raised an eyebrow at me but just nodded.

'That's very kind of you Ruby, but remember to take care of yourself.'

He muttered to himself briefly before wandering off.

Rob was always a man of few words, and tried to avoid any emotional conversations where possible. But it was always evident that he cared for his staff and wanted to make sure that everyone remained happy at work. Ever since his wife had died, he had reverted into himself even more, as though the only light in his life had been squashed out. Vicky, with her marital problems, had jumped at the opportunity to seduce the mildly attractive middle-aged man. I would have felt sorry for her husband Ben, but the looks he had thrown my way at last year's Christmas party had suggested to me that he was doing the dirty himself as well. They truly did deserve each other.

TWO WEEKS LATER

'It's incredible, she's completely healed up, as though there had never been anything wrong.'

Sarah gawked at the X-rays on the screen. I stared at the X-rays, unsure of what I was witnessing, and then back at the chilled-out feline lying across the examination table, looking smug. Rubbing a hand through her auburn ponytail, she could only shrug at me, having no idea how to explain it.

'You know what, I'm not even going to question it, just thank god for that.'

Anticipating the end of the consult, Saffie jumped back into her box. I thanked the vet, paid the ridiculous bill again, and took Saffie home.

'Right Saffie, I'm going out tonight so we need to pick a good dress for me.'

I smiled as I opened the wardrobe, and Saffie lay on the bed relaxing and watching me. I fingered through the various dresses tutting and sighing as I struggled to determine which I wanted to wear. I finally whipped out a short black dress that finished above the knee and had a relatively low-cut front. Saffie purred and rolled onto her back in approval. I span side to side in the mirror, assessing every lump and curve before nodding acceptance of the dress. Then began the arduous task of doing my hair and makeup. The girls were picking me up at seven, so I had just thirty minutes to finish getting ready. I settled on having my wavy hair natural, some black eyeliner and mascara, and some red lipstick. The car pulled up promptly on time, and I squashed myself in the back of the car next to Marie. Faye's boyfriend had kindly offered to drive us all.

'Ready ladies?'

Faye turned to look at me, Marie, and Carly.

'Oh yes!'

We all said in unison. As we pulled away, I saw Saffie watching from the window, and could have sworn she looked worried.

'Right girls, I've got some news.'

Faye announced as we all sat around the table in the bar Nightmare. My wine glass hovered near my lips.

'Matt has asked me to marry him!'

To which we all erupted in to squeals of excitement for our friend. She then produced the engagement ring and slid it onto her finger for us all to see. I had always been jealous of Faye, her beautifully tall and naturally slim figure was a dream.

'And also, I want to ask all three of you to be my bridesmaids.'

It's hard to say who teared up first, but we were all desperately fanning our hands to prevent tears from creating mascara streaks.

'Oh my god Faye, we have been waiting for this moment for you!'

Marie wrapped her arms around Faye, and then we all seemed to pile on to the embrace. Wiping her own eyes, Faye composed herself.

'Right girls, we need a round of shots to celebrate!'

'I am on it!'

I volunteered, shooting up from my seat, credit card at the ready.

I headed straight for the bar, squeezing past various people in the crowded club. Glancing back at the table I smiled warmly as I saw my best friends laughing and squealing. We had all been waiting for Matt to ask Faye to marry him, it had been only 2 years but the guy was smitten from the moment he had set eyes on her. Marie and Carly were already married. It suddenly dawned on me, I was the only one left single. My mildly intoxicated mind drifted briefly back to Brendon, the love of my life, or at least my youth. Brendon and I had been together for 5 years, and after that length of time, I had needed to give up on the hope that he would ever commit to me. Brendon had broken my heart a year ago, but I still hadn't managed to move on enough to establish a real relationship again. I had had flings, but couldn't bring myself to try to connect with someone in the way that I had with Brendon. Shaking myself, I zoned back into the club and the 'night out' vibe I had so desperately wanted. The loud music drummed heavily in my ears.

Once I finally got to the front of the bar, I pressed myself against it so that my breasts pushed upwards into view, and I was almost immediately served. I ordered 8 shots for us, sure that I would regret it in the morning, but uncaring. As I arrived back at the table, the girls cheered, ready to down the shots and then head to the dancefloor. The alcohol warmed my core, and my head span blissfully as I danced with the girls, in what I hoped was actually in time with the music. I felt a pair of hands grab my waist, and I assumed it was Marie who wasn't in front of me, but when I turned to offer her a cheesy grin, I realised it was not her. Instead, two beautiful greying green eyes penetrated through me.

'Woah, he's gorgeous!'

I heard Carly shout.

'Hey, handsome.'

My words slurred as I allowed myself a moment to take in his abnormally attractive face. His complexion was quite pale, but I put that down to the shit lighting in the club. He had short cropped hair, almost as dark as Saffie's fur. A sensual smile spread across his face.

'Hey, beautiful.'

His breath tickled as he whispered in my ear.

'Want to come with me?'

His hand gently began sliding down my arm. Something in my head shouted no, but that voice was drowned out by desire that rushed through me. I couldn't tell if it was the alcohol or something else, but my head felt fuzzy and light as I allowed this beautiful man to lead me through the crowded dance floor and toward an exit. I briefly heard the girls cheering as we left. I felt like my head was trying to warn me of something, some sort of danger, but my body just followed his lead. We stepped outside, and he led me slightly away from the club's back door before pushing me seductively against the wall. He looked into my eyes, and that nagging voice in my head became silenced. His lips interlocked with mine in a passionate, hungry frenzy before he started making his way down, kissing my chin and neck.

Suddenly, a sharp sting erupted in my neck, and an uncomfortable warmth spread through my throat. It took a moment before I realised the freak had bitten me. I tried to push against him but he was solid and unmoving. I tried to scream but nothing came out. My head started to spin, even more than the alcohol-induced vertigo.

I could feel myself becoming weak, but I refused to give up as I kept trying to force my body to fight. Finally, my body listened and my knee thrust upwards, straight into the freak's groin. His teeth scraped out of my neck as he doubled over, moaning loudly in pain. Instinctively I grabbed a fistful of his hair and smashed his face into my knee, before shoving him on his back. My hand grasped at my neck, trying to put pressure on the bleeding. To my right, a flash of light erupted, and I used my other hand to shield my eyes.

'Grab him!'

A booming voice commanded. I lowered my shielding hand to see three people marching towards us. All three seemed solely focussed on the freak that I had briefly disabled. As though he sensed danger, he leapt up and ran at the trio. With a speedy disarming, the only woman of the trio had my attacker on his knees and cuffed. Were they police? They appeared briefly content with their capture, but then their focus moved on to me. Another sense of danger seemed to ring alarm bells in my head, but this time my mind was ready to listen. These three were not in uniform and actually did not look anything like police. In fact, their pointed ears and deadly eyes seemed to make them look particularly inhuman.

The two men began to make their way towards me, and I felt my legs buckling as I stumbled backward, hand still clamped on my bleeding neck. I heard a grumble behind me, and to my complete shock, what appeared to be a panther leapt forward, growling and hissing. Maybe it was the blood loss causing me to imagine things, but the panther turned briefly to give me a look and nodded at me. Saffie? The two men seemed to pause and take note of the cat's size. Meanwhile, I found my head beginning to spin even more violently. I willed myself to stay conscious, but the black spots grew until I finally only saw darkness.

CHAPTER TWO

ASH

There was something about the winter time that made me feel peaceful, the bitter cold air that bit through to the bone was almost refreshing. I found myself lost in thought as the king, otherwise known as my father, droned on about his expectations of us, current threats within the realm, and the usual dull updates. I could feel myself fighting the urge to snooze, when all of a sudden Clem burst through the door, gasping and puffing for air whilst expressing a flustered and urgent state of panic. Clem was one of the throne's trusted allies, and mostly a dithering and pathetic waste of air with a loyalty to his self-preservation before anything else. The king had decided that he would be useful enough to keep alive and serving the throne- from the moment he ratted out his fellow goblins to save his own life, and enabled us to further our influence over the realm. Personally, I saw a coward, but who was I to question the king's orders? Though I supposed I had never felt much tolerance towards non-Fae creatures. All types of Fae were inherently similar in their loyalty and morals and that made it easy to accept them. Even the Seelie, whilst I could not bear them or anything that they represented, still had a code of conduct that they lived by. Albeit a ridiculous and primitive one.

'Sire, please forgive me, I bring urgent news and I believed you would want to know immediately, especially whilst the king's guard is here.'

Clem's head remained tipped down, eyes scrunched shut in anticipation of repercussions.

'Well then speak Goblin, do not keep me waiting.'

'Sire, the vampire named Viktor Adley has been located and is currently on a hunt in the human world.'

The king instantly dismissed Clem and began demanding that I arrange the capture of Viktor and deliver him to the court for his sentencing. Viktor was to be charged for the crime of seducing and slaughtering a few Unseelie females and would be facing flames as a result. It was unusual for a vampire of his age to take such a risk, normally those mistakes were made by newbies with no sire to guide them. Perhaps after so many years, he had gone mad. Supposedly Fae blood was the sweetest to them, some had even likened it to a drug. Though, the older vampires tended to be significantly better at controlling their urges. Apparently not in Victor's case.

Once the king had stormed out of the meeting room, I began arranging the guards.

'Aoife and Bran, you are coming with me to retrieve Viktor, and clean up any mess he has made in the human world.'

I dismissed the other guards. Bran and Aoife had been my closest friends and most loyal members of the king's guard for nearly 200 years now, and there was no doubt in my mind that they would lay down their lives to protect me and the Unseelie throne. The king had shown concerns at first when the pair had become betrothed, for fear that their loyalty would be compromised due to their emotional ties to one another. However, I had been able to convince him that they had proven otherwise numerous times. The internal acknowledgment of the length of time that they had served with me brought a near quirk to my lips. We Unseelie were fortunate enough to experience many more years of life than other beings. As a general rule, all Fae lived significantly longer than most other species, but the Unseelie and Seelie had the highest lifespans among the Fae. Though, we also were leaders of the Fae community, so I suppose that would require us to have substantially higher levels of power to remain in such a position.

Following Clem's intel, we took a portal through to a club in the human world. The neon sign 'Nightmare' glowed and I could practically hear Aoife's internal groaning and Bran's eyes rolling. We had outgrown the excitement of visiting the human world many years ago, and now it meant more hassle and extra work. The humans weren't allowed to know about any form of supernatural- the pathetically sensitive creatures would never be able to handle it. Therefore, we the Fae, often had to mop up when there was a risk of exposure.

'Are we going in?'

Bran's voice already sounded resigned. He had even less tolerance than me when it came to being in the human world. Aoife and I, on our first few visits to the human world, had found it amusing to behold the pitiful creatures and their pointless lives. Bran, on the other hand, was always disinterested in them and keen to leave. Of course, our interest had died out rather quickly. We were now just as bored of the place and its inhabitants as he was.

'You two head around the back and wait for him to bring his meal out, I will head in and ensure that he makes it outside to feed.'

Aoife and Bran seemed to be grateful for this and quickly sped off for the back of the club. Taking a deep breath, I made my way into the bar. The smell of humans was overwhelming, and I had to focus hard to scan the sea of dull and brainless lesser beings. Viktor stood out relatively easily, and I could see him making his move on a young inebriated human girl. Supernaturals often had an alluring effect on humans, but vampires particularly harnessed the skill due to their predatory nature. I monitored as he began to lead her off the dance floor and headed in the direction of the back door. I doubled back through the front and made my way around the outside of the building where Aoife and Bran were waiting. I nodded at them, indicating that he was on his way out.

Viktor had his teeth in the girl before we realised that there was a side door that he must have slipped her through instead. Neither of them seemed to notice us as we came into view, but we were in time to witness the unexpected and feisty fight back that the human gave out. There was something unusual about the girl, the way she fought back was too instinctive and natural. A mere human should definitely not have been able to get the upper hand on a vampire, particularly not one like Viktor. It would have been significantly easier if I were able to send a sharp ice blast at him to immobilise him, but that would have been against the rules. Rules that stopped humans from finding out about us. Structure and order, that was our purpose, and that meant keeping the delicate little humans in the dark about the big scary world.

I motioned forward, and we marched out towards them,

ready to take control of the situation. I gave the command to contain the vamp, but as he recognised our presence, he sprung up from the floor and charged at us. Aoife was speedy in disarming and cuffing him. That was one part of the job done. The girl had witnessed too much, and whilst it wasn't a pleasant task, we had a duty to protect the supernatural world. Bran and I both stepped forward at the same time, ready to give the frightened mortal a peaceful ending. I took in the alarmed look in her eyes, as she suddenly seemed to register we were another threat and not her saviours. Behind her, I could hear a rumbling of feral feline warnings. A black panther jumped out and stepped protectively in front of her. A familiar. Whatever was left of my cold heart warmed slightly. Mine had been a delicate little wren in one form, and a ferocious eagle in another. I had named him Rio. I fought to squash my memories back down into the place where I had buried them. I couldn't afford to think of him. Not now. Not ever. He was gone.

Do not even think about it.

Her voice growled within our minds. Obviously, the whole event and the blood loss was too much for the human as she swiftly hit the floor, unconscious. I could feel Aoife and Bran eyeing me, waiting for orders obediently, but I was at a loss on what to do. The girl was human, or so she appeared, but only someone supernatural would be able to obtain a familiar. I decided to engage the feline and try to establish what was going on.

What is your name familiar?

What's yours?

Her response was laced with sarcasm, clearly aware that a Fae would not give out their name to a stranger, particularly one who may be a threat. However, this was the part where I could take back some control.

I am the Unseelie Prince.

I watched as the cat suddenly drew back in a panic at the recognition of my title. Feeling smug I went to take another step forward, but this was where she reminded me what she was. Her hair stood on end, and her teeth bared as another growl rumbled.

It may have escaped your attention but I am Ruby Goodall's familiar and I will not allow you to harm her, prince or not, I will stop you if you take another step.

A mild sense of respect overcame me, something I rarely felt, and I felt my attack stance relax instinctively. Whilst I was fully aware I could easily slay her, I found myself unwilling to. This creature was definitely bonded to the human, which was something I would need to investigate, but based on the current surroundings I knew that this was neither the time nor the place.

Your human has been drained by a vampire, and that blood loss will be dangerous for her.

The familiar's eyes drifted to the girl lying on the floor, concern evident, so I continued.

I could help her.

Why would you do that?

Because we need to leave before someone comes out here and sees us, and the bite marks on her neck will cause suspicion. If you won't allow me to do my job properly, then at least allow me to clear up the mess in a different way.

The feline nodded reluctantly, overwhelmed by worry for her human. I could feel Bran and Aoife staring in confusion at me, as I moved to the girl's side and touched my fingers to her bleeding neck. I knew that I would be grilled for not killing the girl and her familiar, but that was a problem for later. Under my touch, her skin started to heal over. One positive was that the process of siring a new vampire had not occurred. The human had not had chance to ingest vampire blood, so she was spared from that curse. I then moved my hand to her head.

What are you doing now?

The untrusting familiar hissed at me, still in an attack stance.

I'm taking away tonight's memory, we don't want a human remembering any of this.

I felt my powers and strength weaken as I healed her. Healing was not a power that was naturally mine, and so it would take me some time to get over such an exertion. My mother had been fond of healing, and had gifted me her amethyst just prior to her death. She had claimed that a witch had offered it to her, long ago, as a measure of gratitude for saving their coven. The healing stone was able to channel my ice magic and repurpose it to bring forth a healing power. There were of course limitations to it, it could only heal the more simple of wounds. It was also incredibly draining for the user, which is why it was a rarity that I used it. Even with its limited uses I still felt a level of comfort keeping it on my person.

CHAPTER THREE

RUBY

My eyes fluttered open, and immediately I felt an overwhelming pounding in my head. Thank goodness it was Saturday. Saffie, realising I had woken, made her way up the bed to greet me. Her dainty paws padded lightly up beside me and she sat beside my head. Something felt strange and I couldn't put my finger on what it was. One thing I was certain of; I needed coffee. Groaning and dragging my body out of bed, I scratched my scalp trying to remember the night's events. I could remember up until kissing some guy, but after that the night seemed to be blank. The fact that he wasn't in my house suggested I had managed to make it home alone, and in theory, shouldn't have to face any severe regrets, but I just couldn't ditch the uneasy feeling I had twisting in my stomach. It was as though there was an itch in my brain that I couldn't scratch when I tried to remember. Saffie seemed to be following and monitoring my every move. It was getting annoying.

'Stop being a creeper, Saff, there's already food in your bowl.'

I mumbled at her. Almost as if she understood, she went to the front room and sat on the sofa, eyes still tracking my movements though.

After a nearly rejuvenating shower, I stood in the mirror brushing my hair, when suddenly I had a memory flash of teeth biting into my neck. My hand clasped at my neck in response, and whilst there was no mark visible, I realised how sore it felt there. From the tenderness, there should have been a large amount of bruising spread over the whole right side of my neck and throat.

'What kind of weird stuff did I take part in last night?'

Grabbing my phone, I rang Faye.

'Hey love, how's your head this morning?'

She sounded annoyingly chipper for someone who should have been hanging out of her arse.

'Don't ask. I need a run-through of what the hell happened last night.'

'From which point?'

'Well, I remember kissing some insanely attractive man, but unfortunately, I'm blank after that. Seeing as he's not here this morning, I'm guessing I did something off-putting that I can be reasonably ashamed about?'

'Yeh, I don't actually know why he disappeared, but you came back in the club happy and continued dancing with us. The really shameful behaviour was executed by Carly who attempted to climb the bar to dance. We then got kicked out, so I called Matt to come and get us.'

Faye was clearly tucking into breakfast based on the chewing noises. Wow. I wished I could remember Carly's moment of madness.

'That's insane.'

Faye continued to talk about the night for a bit longer, before moving on to her engagement. Unfortunately, she was unable to provide any details that helped me to decipher what had occurred with the hot stranger, and the mysterious bite memory.

Throughout the day I continued to wrack my brain, but was unsuccessful at restoring any further memories. Saffie seemed to be behaving more weirdly than usual; watching me intensely, constantly. As the evening began drawing to a close and I finished my dinner, I watched Saffie jump down from the sofa in front of me. Suddenly my head felt as though it was getting hotter, and my mind began racing through the events last night. My knees hit the ground, and my fingers wound into my hair as I gripped my throbbing head. Tears streaked down my face as the pain became unbearable. After what felt like an eternity, the pain started to ease off and I was able to catch my breath. Finally, the memories returned to me, and I found myself pinned to the sofa and staring wide-eyed at my cat. No, not my cat. What the hell even was she? She seemed to understand as she looked nervously around.

'What are you?'

The words barely came out. Saffie's head dipped slightly and a voice appeared in my head. At first, I struggled to understand if I was imagining it in my panic-stricken state.

Ruby, I know this is very confusing, but I need you to allow me to explain.

When I didn't answer she continued.

I am what is known as a familiar, and you are my soul mate.

Her eyes burned into mine, and a sense of calm washed over me.

'What is a familiar? And how can my soul mate be a cat? I may have joked about becoming a crazy cat lady in the future, but this is way too messed up!'

The words came out so frantic and fast, to the point that I could barely recognise my own voice.

A familiar is a spirit companion, who attaches to a supernatural being and forms an unbreakable bond based on the interlinking of their souls. The night I jumped in your window I was being attacked, and my instincts drew me to you. Your soul called to mine when I was in danger, and yours did the same to me when you were being attacked last night.

I felt as though my eyes were bulging from their sockets, my mouth had become desperately dry, and I couldn't seem to form any sort of response.

I understand this is a lot to take in Ruby, but I also know that you know I'm telling you the truth. I will protect you until I release my last breath.

Despite everything seeming to suggest that I needed to be admitted to a psychiatric hospital, I had a gut instinct to believe Saffie.

'If this is true, then why are you attached to me? I'm not supernatural, whatever that even is.'

Saffie regarded me for a minute before answering.

I don't have an answer for that, you must have something supernatural in you because we can't bond to humans, but I don't know what you are Ruby.

Saffie seemed genuinely as perplexed as she said. My mind felt as though it was ready to burst as I began to question everything I knew.

Saffie spent time explaining to me that she could morph between a domestic cat to a black panther, and that all familiars were different. She touched a bit further on our psychic bond too, and explained that she communicates through telepathy. Apparently, there's a sort of open channel that all supernaturals can communicate with familiars through if in close contact, and a private one for just us. She also admitted that the reason I wasn't freaking out more was due to her 'influence' that she was holding over me, though I wasn't complaining about the mental drugging because I would definitely have been on the floor by now without it.

'So, was that a vampire that bit me the other night?'

Her feline head bobbed in a nod at my question.

'Vampires really are sexy like in the movies.'

I had never seen a cat roll its eyes until now.

'So what were the other three? Aliens?'

I couldn't tell if Saffie appreciated my humorous responses but it was the only way I could force myself to cope with the completely life- changing information.

They were Fae.

There was a hint of distaste as she said this.

Or faeries if you prefer. Essentially the dictators of the supernatural world. Completely uptight arseholes if you ask me.

My shock should have been in response to the crazy knowledge that faeries were real, but really I couldn't believe Saffie was calling someone an arsehole. Reading my mind, she added

I've spent too much time around you already.

By the time I crawled into bed, I felt completely over-whelmed and exhausted. Saffie hesitated in the doorway, unsure if I would allow her to sleep on the bed as she previously did, but I motioned her up and I could practically hear her breathe a sigh of relief. Darkness flooded my mind quickly after my head hit the pillow.

The following day flowed relatively easily, I had decided to do my shift at work, despite my overwhelming urge to hide under my bed covers for the entire day. It did help me to be distracted. Finally, in the evening, I felt like a bottle of wine was deserved so I headed to the shop down the road. Saffie had offered to come with me, but I needed the time by myself to gather my thoughts without fear of being listened to. Whilst Saff had assured me she could only hear the thoughts that I directed to her, I still had become concerned over what went on in my head, just in case she could hear. Something was soothing about a solitary walk in the night. The cold air was refreshing and the beautiful night sky gave me a welcomed distraction. I felt comfortable and relaxed for the first time, that was up until the walk back home. At first, I felt a strange sense of someone watching me, and then movements from the corners of my eyes sent my heart pounding in my chest. My gut instinct told me there was a danger around, and after all I had learned in the last 24 hours I definitely was listening to it. I picked up the pace, and had to wonder if the thudding of my heart was actually as loud as it seemed to me. I can't say for sure what came over me, but I would guess that the fight instinct is to blame, I paused and spun around to where I could sense my follower's presence.

'I'm not running from you, so come out and face me you creeper!'

Instantly I regretted my decision to suddenly become brave, as a figure stepped out of the shadows.

He stepped towards me, a menacing smile playing on his lips. My eyes dragged over the most perfect creature I had ever come across. His slim, but muscular shape was evident from the way his t-shirt clung to him. He could have almost passed for a model-like human, except that the dark mop of hair was not enough to hide his pointed Fae ears. It was peculiar to see that they dressed like humans. Not that I had ever particularly thought about faeries, but if I had then I would have expected more of a historical fashion.

'You're a brave little human really, aren't you.'

He mocked. Whilst my head screamed at me not to do it, my stubbornness and sarcastic nature seemed to take great offense at his words.

'Maybe you're the brave one coming after me without your back-up.'

His eyebrow rose in surprise, but his vicious smirk didn't falter. My heart was pounding in my chest so hard that I was almost sure it would crack a rib, and I could only pray that he couldn't hear it. Although, I got the distinct impression that I stank of fear and panic as he looked at me like a lion stalking its prey.

'My associates are currently ensuring the safe detainment of your familiar. I took the easier option and decided to take care of the pesky human who has somehow tumbled into a world that doesn't concern her.'

My mind raced as I took in his words. Saffie was in danger. I suddenly realised that's why I had sensed the danger in the first place, it must have been Saffie warning me.

'If you hurt her I swear...'

He held a hand up to pause me.

'The familiar is unharmed, the king wants you both alive.'

I span on my heel and followed my instinct to run. I made it to all of about five paces before a hand wrapped around my arm and yanked me back. I attempted to peel his long fingers off of me, but to no avail. My captor just rolled his eyes at me. As we locked eyes I felt sheer terror flood me.

His cold, hardened eyes assessed me with an underlying hint of... curiosity?

'Are those really necessary?'

I moaned as a pair of rings in illuminating blue wrapped around my wrists; some sort of supernatural handcuff. He ignored me, instead turning his attention ahead of us, and began creating a circling motion with his hand. Out of nowhere, a bright green light appeared in front of us.

'It's a portal to the Fae realm.'

He clarified, noticing my shock and confusion.

'I don't think I want...'

I was cut short when he simply dragged me into the bright green portal. It's hard to describe the feeling of a portal, but I would liken it to the way your stomach drops when you fall from a height. Needless to say, I stumbled to the ground on the other side and found myself mildly grateful that my captor had such a firm grip on my arm, otherwise, I would have face-planted snow. He tutted and dragged me upwards so that I was back upright.

'Wow chivalry really is dead.'

I muttered, and I could have sworn I saw him almost smile.

The icy landscape in front of me was breath-taking. Snow crunched under my feet, layered the trees, and coated the castle before us.

'Woah.'

The word escaped as I took in the magnificent structure. I had never been interested in architecture before, but the castle was one building I was fascinated by. Even layered with snow the grounds surrounding it looked simply magical. I blinked hard, expecting to wake up back in my bedroom. Surely this place could not actually be real?

'It's like a fairy tale castle, although I suppose it would be if it holds a load of faeries.'

I couldn't stifle my giggles. I was the only one to laugh. Insane. I was going insane.

'Do I get to know your name, or shall I just keep calling you the creep who kidnapped me?'

He did not reply, or even look at me for that matter. Instead, he marched me toward the beautiful but terrifying castle ahead, and the frozen environment mixed with silence made it even more eerie. As we entered, I felt Saffie calling to me.

Are you okay Saf?

Yes, are you in the castle?

Just walking down a spooky hallway now.

He's bringing you to the Unseelie king. We don't have long, just let me advise you before you answer anything. The Unseelie are cunning and cruel and will kill us both if you make a wrong move.

Not filling me with any form of confidence here Saf!

Her voice went silent and we arrived at a large wooden door. I quickly turned to my captor

'Are there any chances of you taking pity on me and letting me go?'

Without responding to my question, he pulled me forward and pushed me through the door.

Entering the room, all I could think was; this is how it ends, in a faery castle, in my loungewear clothes. Immediately my eyes found Saffie. She was in her panther form, held down with large silver chains and guarded by several pointy-eared freaks. Anger bubbled in my chest.

Don't react.

Her voice sounded in my head. Swallowing down my anger, I allowed my captor to drag me forward. An attractive, middle aged looking man sat upon a throne ahead, a stone-cold stare piercing through me. I felt my blood run cold from the disgust and cruel intent hitting me in the face. My captor shoved me to my knees in front of the throne, and I could feel everyone's eyes on me.

'Ruby Goodall, welcome to the Fae realm.'

His smile was completely disingenuous, my mouth went dry at the sound of his voice.

Saf, my spidey sense is tingling.

Only a few weeks with you, and yet I'm ashamed to say I understand you. I don't know what he is planning but it can't be good.

'I am the Unseelie king, and I have summoned you here as you appear to have slipped through the cracks until now. We, the Unseelie, monitor the supernatural world and maintain order among it, and you, my dear, seem to have been hiding from us.'

'I think hiding may be the wrong choice of words, more that I'm a human whose life has been completely rear-ended and set on fire!'

A terrified and almost hysterical chuckle erupted from me. Surely I was overdue a breakdown by now?

'My stray cat is actually some sort of spirit thing that can become a panther, I got bitten by a vampire, and now I've been captured by a bloody faery. Trust me, I've not been hiding, you have all just invaded my life for a reason that none of us seem to know.'

I instantly regretted my outburst. Saffie's voice was silent in my head, but I could sense her fearful anticipation, and the room was silently watching me. Why was I never capable of keeping my thoughts internal? After a minute the king finally spoke again.

'Well, you certainly reek of human fear.'

With that, there were chuckles around the room. My anger started to bubble again, how dare these sadistic freaks laugh at me? Before I could have another outburst, he continued.

'If you have a familiar then there is something supernatural about you, and I for one am intrigued to know what it is, so that we can reasonably decide your fate.'

The end of his sentence was dripping with cruel excitement, and I got the feeling he was hoping for a reason to make sure my fate was painful.

'My son here, the Prince, will find you and your familiar a secure room for your stay here.'

I followed the king's eyeline to see my captor nodding in response. Not good. An amused smirk appeared on his face as he took in my reddening cheeks.

'So where are we going your highness?'

I was back to feeling stupidly brave and sarcastic. I was probably going to die anyway right? He turned his head and gave me an odd look at my question.

'Your Highness?'

'Is that not the correct term here? I've never been in the presence of any kind of royalty, especially not pointy-eared royalty.'

He shook his head without replying, and instead created an uncomfortable silence. With no further words, we climbed a staircase and entered another hallway, this time with numerous doors that I could only guess were bedrooms. Around a third of the way down, we halted.

'This is your room.'

His tone had become bored but mildly hostile again as he unlocked the door.

My shock must have been amusing to him because I heard him try to hide a laugh with a cough.

'Were you expecting a prison cell or something?'

'Actually yes.'

My voice barely sounded, as I took in the king-size, four-poster bed, and absolutely beautiful traditional décor. It was the look I could only dream of bringing to my bedroom in my small two-bed terraced house back home.

'Your familiar will be brought up here shortly. Tomorrow morning someone will collect you.'

'Collect me for what?'

'For testing of course.'

His sadistic smile made me shiver uncontrollably. With that, he departed the room, and I was left in the beautifully bitter room.

Eventually, Saffie came into the room, back in her domestic feline form.

'You have no idea how glad I am to see you.'

I sighed as I jumped up from the deliciously comfortable bed.

Missed me?

Are you okay? Did they hurt you?

No, they questioned me rather pleasantly actually, compared to what I expected from the Fae.

Oh, well, that's good then I suppose.

We need to talk about tomorrow.

What about it?

I could feel the sweat forming on my forehead, already aware it was going to be horrible.

The elders are going to be... examining you, to find out what exactly you are.

What are the elders?

They are ancient Fae, no one knows how old, but they will be assessing you to find out what you are, other than human. If you are proved as anything other than Fae, you are fair game to kill.

But I'm a human, I have nothing else going on!

I could actively feel my pulse quickening, as I was becoming even more certain I would be sentenced to death tomorrow.

Ruby, you can't be completely human. As the king said, I can't bond with a human, you must have something super-natural somewhere in your lineage. Please think, can you remember anything unusual, any odd family stories?

Oh yes, I remember the stories of dear old grandma and grandpa the faeries!

I spat sarcastically. I could practically hear Saffie's eyes rolling as I paced and gestured dramatically in front of her.

Ruby, I'm worried because I can't protect you.

Saf, if I'm going to be executed tomorrow, promise me you will run, just get away from there and run for your life.

Ruby, I am destined to serve you and protect you until I die, there is not an option for me to run. We will go down together fighting these pointy-eared freaks.

Tears formed in my eyes at my new found best friend, who had already become a part of me, and I wrapped her in a cuddle. Eventually, we settled into the beautiful, but un-homely, bed and drifted off to sleep.

CHAPTER FOUR

RUBY

A harsh knocking on the door awoke me from my relatively peaceful and dream-free slumber. Bursting through the door, a Fae female entered my room, and naturally, I pulled the cover up higher in a defensive movement. Squinting my eyes, adjusting to being awake, I vaguely recognised the woman from the night at the club.

'Get up human, we have to be downstairs shortly.'

Her annoyed look showed she had been forced into being my wake-up call and chaperone.

'Wow, not even a lie in before I'm murdered.'

I chuckled without humour. Saffie yawned and stretched out beside me.

Who's this bundle of joy?

Aoife, one of the king's guard, and one of the Prince's closest allies.

Saffie mirrored my pretend nonchalance at our fate to come. We may have been terrified, but we had already agreed not to let them have the satisfaction of seeing it.

'Get up before I make you.'

Aoife's tone was curt. I glared in her direction and pulled myself out of bed, still in yesterday's clothes. She rolled her eyes at my appearance.

'It's hard to be prepared when you've been kidnapped.'

I muttered profanities under my breath regarding her distaste towards me.

'You're very sarcastic for a human facing likely death.'

Her words should have sounded sarcastic, I'm sure, but instead they sounded inquisitive.

'How else would you expect me to deal with it?'

She seemed to genuinely consider my question.

'I expected begging and crying.'

Her answer was brutally honest, which under different circumstances may have elicited a smile from me.

'I'd rather die than beg you pointy-eared crazies.'

I laughed, and Saffie mewed in agreement. Much to my surprise, Aoife laughed as well, a genuine hearty laugh.

'I am actually hopeful you're part Fae, you make me laugh.'

Saffie gave me an impressed look, and I couldn't form a reasonable response so settled on a shrug.

Aoife led us back down the stairs and into the room where we had met the king the day before. The king was not present this time, but seven robed figures stood in a semi-circle before me. I couldn't see their faces, but their presence created an eerie feeling and a sense of impending doom.

'Welcome Miss Goodall.'

One of the figures spoke, but it was impossible to say which one it was. In unison they lifted their heads, to reveal a sight that I couldn't have ever been ready for. I clenched my jaw and sucked in a breath, In my best attempt not to scream. Their greying skin barely covered their skeleton faces, and their eyes were incredibly sunken. In essence, they looked like decaying corpses, and I half expected to see a body part fall off one of them. The pointed tips of their ears were the only aspect that looked even remotely Fae. My stomach had started churning, and I had to swallow down the threat of a nervous vomit. It was likely I was supposed to reply to their greeting, but I couldn't physically form any words. Aoife had moved away from me and made her way to the side of the room with what I could only assume was the rest of the king's guard, as the prince was stood at the front of the group. A nudge of my leg drew my attention to Saffie who had joined me. I tried to search for our channel so I could speak to her, but it was silent.

'You will not be able to speak to your familiar at this time.'

One of the elders informed me. Their voices were so ominous that they caused me to tremble uncontrollably, and the lack of Saffie's mental presence made me significantly more alone in this.

'Ruby Goodall, you are here so we can determine what class of supernatural being you are related to so that judgment for your crimes can be appropriately dealt with.'

'Crimes?'

I received a sharp claw to the leg from Saffie for my outburst, indicating I needed to keep my mouth shut. Thankfully the skeleton men, otherwise known as the elders, ignored me and continued.

'Come forward.'

I obeyed cautiously, looking for other exits that I could make a run for. To my alarm, they began circling me until I was in the middle of them all. They joined hands and began chanting. My breath caught first and my hands instinctively grasped at my throat, as if to manually squeeze air in and out. The burning sensation in my empty lungs grew until I dropped to my knees, eyes watering. Then the second wave of pain came. All of the hairs on my arms stood on end as a wave of heat erupted across my flesh. It started from the skin and penetrated through, digging deeper and deeper until I felt as though my entire body was on fire. With the lack of breath, I couldn't even scream, but tears came thick and fast, streaming down my face and pooling on the floor that my forehead was now pressed to. I couldn't even beg them to stop. I had no idea what they were chanting, it was just a background noise, far overshadowed by the worst pains I had ever felt. Just when I thought I was going to slip into unconsciousness, and was pretty much praying for death, a cooling breeze whipped across me and extinguished the heat. The tight restriction around my lungs released, and I erupted into a coughing fit, sucking in the delicious oxygen with more gratitude than I'd ever thought possible.

'The test is done.'

The elders all said in unison. I remained curled up in a foetal position, unable to collect myself. My body still felt the sting of the cruel process, and my mind... well that felt shattered by it.

'The girl has Fae blood coursing through her.'

The elder's circle began to dissipate. I wanted to take in their words, to ask questions, but I was not capable of processing anything. I felt Saffie appear at my side and she nuzzled her head against me.

To my surprise, it was Aoife who first made a move towards me. Expecting the worst I flinched away as her hand extended down to me.

'Let me help you.'

Her words were firm but there was a mild kindness I hadn't anticipated. My shaky hand nervously gripped onto hers, and she pulled me to my feet relatively effortlessly.

Using the last bit of strength I had left I managed to hold myself upright, though my legs did not feel stable. The prince had stared at me for a moment, furrowed his brow, and then disappeared out of the room. One of the other guards came forward, a hesitant and slightly forced smile on his lips as he approached us.

'Ruby, this is my husband Bran.'

Aoife nodded her head as he reached us. He uncomfortably offered his hand to shake, and it took an alarming amount of effort to will my hand to meet his. Before I could muster up the energy to ask Aoife and Bran any questions, the door flung open, and in marched the king, the prince, and some other members of the king's guard. They all headed straight for me.

'Ruby Goodall, I hear you became a very fortunate woman just moments ago.'

The king sneered, and whilst my head wanted to reply sarcastically, my body seemed to have more self-preservation instincts, and my lips remained tightly pressed together.

'As you have been proven to have Fae blood running through you, you will be pardoned. However, we are yet to determine what a Fae girl was doing being born into a human family and in the human world.'

The last part was muttered rather than dictated, and so it seemed he was more speaking to himself, perplexed by the situation.

'Aoife, please take Miss Goodall to her bedroom for her to change, the smell of fear and sweat is unbearable.'

If I hadn't been completely wiped out, I would have

been fuming. Instead, I simply followed obediently behind Aoife, feeling that the last of my self-respect and dignity had left the building. I couldn't meet the Prince's eyes as we walked past, but I could feel him watching me, most likely smirking that arrogant smile of his.

ASH

The image of Ruby writhing on the floor in agony played over and over in my mind. Thankfully I had only ever experienced the Elders' magic once before, a few hundred years ago, but there was no forgetting it. The way her face had contorted from defensive caution to desperate pleading, her tears had come thick and heavy in her silent cries. I couldn't have helped even if I had wanted to. I did find myself harbouring mild respect for the girl. She had faced the elders and survived it. Not only survived it, but came out of it with her mind still relatively intact. Perhaps there was more to her than there appeared. Maybe her faerie side was stronger than anyone was giving her credit for. If she was more Fae than she was showing, was she aware? The thoughts continued to circle my head, more questions arose than my mind could solve.

It was my father that snapped me out of my all consuming vicious cycle of thoughts regarding the enigma that was Ruby Goodall. He marched into my bed chamber, full of purpose and looking mildly concerned. The closing of the door behind him indicated a private chat was about to happen, and that usually meant bad news. I regarded my father with the inflated level of respect that he demanded.

'I was summoned to a meeting with the elders.'

He paced in front of my bed where I sat. I placed my book down, ready to listen.

'They have given me reason to be concerned over our human guest. It appears that they have discovered more details about her Fae background.'

He paused for dramatic effect, which worked as I felt my pulse begin to quicken with the suspense.

'It appears Miss Goodall is a descendent from Titania's blood line. We must be wary of her.'

The king's forehead had become increasingly creased as he talked, showing more stress than he would have liked visible.

'It is imperative that no one else finds out about her heritage, and we need to establish if she is aware or has any abilities that could pose a threat to us.'

'I'm surprised you haven't already had her killed.'

My words came out as flat as I had intended them to be, but I was genuinely surprised. We both knew what risk Titania's bloodline could pose to us, and my father was not the type to take unnecessary risks out of the kindness of his heart. In fact to even imagine my father had a heart was comical.

'The elders have just announced in front of an audience that the girl is part Fae, to execute her without a good reason would be suspicious and the rebels would jump on the opportunity to turn more against us.'

I nodded in understanding. Whilst it had been just shy of two hundred years, some people had not forgotten the past and we were well aware of small revolt groups that had formed here and there over the realm. The groups were minor mostly and easily squashed out when discovered, but if they saw the Unseelie King killing 'innocent' faeries then it would worsen the situation. Her stubbornness and feisty attitude in the face of danger were starting to make a bit more sense now at least. I had never had the displeasure of meeting Titania, but I had seen pictures and my grandfather had drilled into me the story of his greatest battle for the throne. Prior to seizing the throne, my family had been in very high standing, so we were readily accepted by most as the new leaders. The odd few, however, were Titania loyalists to the end and were intent on finding ways to overthrow us.

'We need her closely monitored, which is why you will be making her a 'trainee' of the King's guard.'

My head snapped up at this, he had to be joking?

'You can train her and monitor her progress and report back what you find, if anything.'

'She will be killed in the King's guard.'

'So be it, problem solved. A noble death that no one will question.'

Before I could offer further protest, my father swiftly exited the room, muttering to himself.

RUBY

Once we were back in the room, I could feel Saffie trying to open our telepathic channel, but I blocked her out. I couldn't face talking to anyone. She seemed to get the hint eventually and curled at the end of the bed near my feet. My tears soaked into the pillow freely and silently. I must have fallen asleep at some point as a cough startled me awake, and I shot upright. The prince was leaning against my door frame, arms crossed and his seemingly typical smug look across his face. In my semi-sleepy state, I found my eyes analysing his perfect form a bit too much, and then swiftly realised that was why he was looking smug.

'Enjoying the view human?'

His cocky voice was almost playful again.

'More pondering why you felt it was appropriate to open my bedroom door, and stand there watching me sleep like that. That's an arrestable offense in my world you know.'

'Funnily enough, I don't enjoy spending my time interacting with humans, let alone watching them dribble onto a pillow whilst snoring.'

My cheeks flushed red, had I dribbled? I sneaked a side glance at my pillow. Before I could awkwardly stutter an embarrassed retort, he continued speaking.

'I've come to inform you that you have been upgraded from hostage to trainee.'

'Trainee for what?'

'For joining the king's guard.'

His voice had gone serious, and a glazed-over look appeared in his eyes, which made me feel extra wary.

'Well as kind as that is, I don't really want to be trained thank you, I already have a job and in fact a life. A life which you kidnapped me from.'

His face remained stony and pretty unaccepting.

'It's non-negotiable I'm afraid.'

His monotone indicated that the topic wasn't open for discussion, but that didn't stop me from kicking up a fuss. I leapt out of bed and stormed towards him, he stayed perfectly in place.

'You might be a prince here in bloody faery land, but you are not royalty where I come from. I don't know why you think it's acceptable to abduct a person and then take over their life, but I can assure you that I will not be doing a damn thing for you. Now take me and my cat home!'

A slight hint of humour passed his face which just infuriated me more. My hands were on my hips, and I had tried my best to do the most effective squaring of my shoulders that I could do. Though his relaxed frame towering over me made me realise that I perhaps wasn't as threatening as I had intended to be.

'I think you perhaps misunderstood when I said it was not negotiable. Whilst you are pretty much completely human, there is some Fae blood somewhere in you and we unfortunately have an obligation to.'

He paused, choosing his words carefully.

'Look after you. Clean yourself up and meet me down in the training hall.'

Something about his caution rang alarm bells in my head. Before I could protest further though, he pushed away from the door frame and turned to walk away.

I glared at his back as he walked away, but also couldn't help a cheeky ogle at his behind as well. Clean myself up? A quick look in the mirror explained his harsh comment. Black mascara streaks were dried onto my cheeks, and I could only sigh in further embarrassment before cleaning the disaster that was my face. I didn't even want to acknowledge the likely sweaty odour that I was emitting.

Couldn't have warned me I looked like a horror film?

I glanced at Saffie who was still curled up on the bed, but was monitoring me.

Didn't want to interrupt your angry flow.

I rolled my eyes at her.

Any idea where the training hall is?

She shook her head at me before stretching and jumping down to my side.

Okay then we better go and find it. Hopefully, we will accidentally stumble across a portal home on the way.

Walking down the hall I sucked in some deep breaths and summoned my inner feisty side, it seemed like the only way to avoid a mental breakdown and perhaps stand a chance of surviving. These faeries seemed to thrive off humiliating and scaring me, so it was time to stop giving them what they wanted. If I was part Fae myself, and they were going to force me into training with them, then surely there was a possibility of earning some respect or trust? I only needed enough to get them to relax their grip on me so that I could find a way of escaping. I made my way back down the stairs and suddenly found myself almost walking straight into Aoife.

'Follow me.'

She instructed, span around and began walking off.

'I'm supposed to be going to the training hall.'

My words stuttered as I jogged to catch her up.

'Where do you think I'm taking you?'

She seemed irritated, though I couldn't imagine it was to do with me as she had been fine when I last spoke to her. Just in case though, I stayed quiet and obediently followed. We took another hallway, and then some further stone steps down into a below ground level area of the castle. The dark halls were lit with candles on the walls, and there was an eerie beauty to the place that left me with shivers but also in awe. Eventually, we were led into a large hall. The hall was modern-looking in contrast to the hallways leading to It, and the bright lighting made my eyes sting at first. In one third of it were some torturous looking gym equipment that reminded me why I never had managed more than one session at the gym back home. The other area was bare, which seemed odd. The prince stood In the centre, his face unreadable. He motioned for me to approach him, and nodded to Aoife to join me.

'Right, time to see what instincts we have in there.'

'What do you mean?'

In response, he nodded again at Aoife and stepped away from us. I turned to Aoife and was shocked to see her in a fighting stance, with her fists up in a guarding action.

'We are sparring Ruby. I will take it easy on you don't worry.'

Ruby be careful.

Saffie's voice sounded in my head.

'Ruby get in position.'

The Prince tutted impatiently. Panic starting to course through me, but remembering that I was trying not to show fear, I mirrored Aoife's positioning and focussed on trying to keep my fists from shaking. Aoife started circling around me, and I did my best to keep her in sight. Before I could even register her movement a fist flew at my face and connected with my cheek. I stumbled and grabbed at my face, but then her foot came quickly at my side and smashed into my ribs and sent me flying the other way.

'Get up.'

Sucking in a deep breath, I winced through the pain as I dragged myself back to my feet. Within a second her fist was slamming into my face again, but this time I felt a crunch that created more pain than I could cope with. Things seemed to slow down then. I touched my face and wiped the blood from it. Something inside me snapped, and it was as though a feral instinct took over. I saw her fist coming this time and managed to duck below it before throwing a couple of jabs at her abdomen. As the impact forced her back, and her surprise delayed her response, it gave me a chance to deliver a kick straight to her shins so that her knees buckled beneath her.

A clapping snapped me out of the moment. My hands instantly released from their balled up state, and my injuries began to radiate the increasing pain. My face felt disfigured and my ribs must have been cracked. Aoife smirked from the ground, where she had relaxed back onto her elbows to watch.

'Aoife can you go and get Samira please, I think Ruby would appreciate a quicker healing process than the one her mortal side will provide.'

Aoife obediently rose to her feet and speedily exited the hall at the Prince's instruction, as though nothing had happened. I held back the tears as the pain seared through me, how had Aoife not even broken a sweat?

'How do you feel?'

I gave the Prince a look which I hoped portrayed disgust but with the swelling I could feel building it was hard to know if I could give any expression. When I didn't reply he stopped smiling.

'You have some speed and strength of the Fae, but your human side masks it until your body is under threat and enters fight or flight mode.'

Despite my deteriorating state, I did take a minute to consider this. It made sense. The innate reflexes that over-came me just when I was at a point of my body giving in.

'Like with that vampire.'

My voice came out croaky, the words slightly muffled by my puffed-up mouth. The Prince nodded.

'To be honest, that's where the idea came from. I remembered how you fought Viktor, no human would have managed that, and so I needed to test my theory.'

'So much for Aoife going easy on me.'

I gently fingered the swelling that was forming under my eye. The Prince let out a light chuckle again.

'That was her going easy.'

My eyes would have widened if my face didn't throb too much with any movement.

It felt like a lifetime before Aoife returned, but the clock showed that in reality, it had been just shy of five minutes. By this point though I was wishing she had knocked me unconscious, as the pain was unbearable. Following Aoife into the room was another lady, who I could only guess was Samira. This was instantly confirmed as Aoife introduced us.

'Samira is going to fix you up a bit.'

'Not completely, but enough to help you through.'

Her voice was sweet and gentle, nothing like the other faeries I had met so far. She had dark skin and beautiful long black hair flowing down her back. She was shorter, more petite and child-like in her appearance, in comparison to Aoife. I noticed her ears were not pointed quite like the others also.

'Are you one of the Unseelie too?'

'No, I'm a Nymph.'

She continued to smile sweetly as she pulled out a pot from her pocket, opened the lid and began rubbing a pale green cream over my face. I flinched as her hand came towards my face, but her genuine smile made me relax a bit more and accept her help. After smothering me in the smelly green cream, she placed her hands on either side of my head and closed her eyes. I gave the Prince a curious look, but his face remained focused and unchanged as he watched Samira working on me. At first I couldn't feel any difference, but then a cooling sensation ran over my skin. The burning pain began to melt away, and I could feel the pressure from the various facial swellings decreasing.

'What's a nymph?'

I had begun to start feeling awkward with everyone staring at me and a strange girl's hands stroking my head.

'A different race of faery.'

Aoife replied. No one offered any further information, so I made a mental note to research nymphs later. Once Samira had finished, she opened her eyes and gave me a big grin.

'Much better.'

She handed me a compact mirror from her pocket. Whilst I could appreciate that this must have been an improvement, I couldn't hide the horror at the black eye, bruising spread down both sides of my face, and the split lip. The swellings I had previously felt were gone, but I was definitely not as good as new. Samira must have recognised my shock.

'I know it's not perfect, but I've saved you about a week of healing time.'

Her voice was filled with compassion.

'You've done a great job Samira, thank you for your assistance.'

The prince's softer voice surprised me, but the look he gave me was not as kind. Samira gathered up her items and left the hall, giving me a gentle squeeze on the shoulder as she departed.

'That will do for you today, we will start properly tomorrow. For now, just sit and watch as the others train.'

The prince commanded, and as if on cue the rest of the Kings guards made their way in to the hall. Following the Prince's instructions, they split into pairs and began battling. Aoife was unsurprisingly paired with Bran, her husband, and I watched with amazement as they began 'training'. Knives whizzed around, and blurs of fast movements captivated my interest. I must have been watching with a gormless expression, because I caught the prince glance at me and try not to smile in amusement. The way they all moved was incredible, I had never seen such beauty in aggression. Every movement was calculated and executed with such precision that one could have believed they were dancing, if it weren't for the various weapons being slung around at the same time. Was this what was expected of me? If so, I was going to be a severe disappointment.

They have been born into this lifestyle Ruby.

I hadn't realised that Saffie had come and sat beside me until her voice reminded me that she was in the room. Her words were intended to comfort me but in reality they just made me realise how little I fitted into this life that had been forced upon me. Tears stung my eyes, but I refused to let them out, unwilling to allow the cruel creatures ahead to feel any sort of victory over me.

We need to find a way out of here.

If we run they will just come after us.

Saffie sounded as defeated as I felt

There has to be a way Saf.

I did a little bit of exploring last night when I couldn't sleep. There's a library down the hall from our room. There seemed to be an awful lot of books, varying from history to spells. Maybe we need to do some research.

I had to admit I was impressed with Saffie, and agreed that we would explore the library as soon as we were left alone long enough.

CHAPTER FIVE

RUBY

The next couple of weeks mostly consisted of me having my arse kicked repeatedly, and trying to get in as many punches as I could in the process. Samira had commented how she had never been needed so frequently by one person, which made me feel even more pathetic. The majority of the king's guard mocked me daily and regarded me with a certain level of disgust, but this was just when Aoife, Bran, and the Prince weren't watching. Whilst Aoife seemed to have found a fondness for me, I could tell that Bran was far less trusting and only tolerated me because Aoife had taken a shine. The prince had continued to be a sarcastic dick, but I played the part and obeyed like all of the other good little pointy-eared soldiers. Meanwhile, in the evenings Saffie and I had been sneaking into the library and taking the odd book back to our room to research. So far our research had come up fruitless, but I had learned more about the different types of Fae in the realm which I figured would prove useful.

Saffie had mostly stopped coming with me to my daily duties and instead had spent her time investigating all the nooks and crannies of the castle. I had been given back my mobile phone after my first day, and begrudgingly advised Rob that I would not be returning to the restaurant. He had phoned me and asked me what was wrong, suspicious of my out-of-character behaviour. I had to think on the spot and pretended that I was having some sort of epiphany and had gone traveling. My friends thankfully were too wrapped up in their own lives to even notice that I was no longer in the same world as them. I had never been grateful for being a foster system kid before, but in this instance, it was proving beneficial to have no family searching for me. I had briefly considered phoning for help until I realised that I would be admitted to a psychiatric hospital upon my return to the human world if I began talking about being abducted by faeries.

'Ready for another round today Ruby?'

Oakley, one of the few guards who had decided to be nice to me, playfully jabbed at my arm as we entered the hall for the morning training. There were fewer of us today, some had been sent out on missions from the Prince.

'Remember I'm mostly human, that whole being thrown across the room yesterday has not helped my enthusiasm.'

Oakley nodded, trying to show understanding.

The first half of the day went relatively quickly, but it slowed down significantly after lunch when Oakley and I were assigned the duty of guarding the court room. I witnessed prisoners being dragged into the room for their sentencing and then escorted out afterward. I couldn't hear the court proceedings, so instead Oakley and I took the time to make light conversation and discuss areas of my fighting that I needed to focus on for improvement. When we heard footsteps coming down the hall, we stopped our nattering. As they stepped around the corner I felt the air whip out of me. Him. He must have recognised me instantly because a dark smile crept across his face. His eyes locked with mine, and though my skin was crawling and itching for me to get away, I couldn't stop staring back. He said nothing as the guards escorted him past me and through into the court room. My stomach was churning and I leaned back against the wall to steady myself.

'Are you alright Ruby?'

He touched my arm, eyes full of concern.

'That was the vampire that started all this. He is the reason I'm here.'

The words came out barely audible.

'Viktor will be sentenced to death today.'

He was expecting that to reassure me. It didn't. I forced my face to return a smile to him, though I can imagine it was tight. I desperately wanted to hear the proceedings for his case. I wanted this vampire to be punished, he had ruined my life. It took all of about five minutes before they brought Viktor back out of the room, I assumed the speed meant that the decision was easy. Viktor turned his head and winked at me as the guards dragged him away. Was he going to be released? That was one damn smug look for someone presumed to receive a death sentence. Oakley gave me a reassuring smile, clearly oblivious to Viktor's smug face. Once again my stomach was turning, and my gut feeling said that something bad was going on.

Eventually the working day came to an end, and I felt both physically and emotionally exhausted. There was a distinct difference between me and the Fae in terms of how much we could handle. I was struggling to make it through each day, whereas the others breezed through with a smile and eagerness to do more. As Oakley and I left our position and made our way back in the direction of our rooms, Aoife appeared with an unusually big smile spread across her face.

'It's the last Friday of the month!'

She grinned in a way that I could almost mistake for human.

'I'll be ready in thirty minutes.'

Oakley winked at her.

'What am I missing?'

I questioned, wondering if I was witnessing something I shouldn't be.

'Party night.'

Aoife wiggled her eyebrows at me. This had to be a joke right? These creatures of habit with their regimented lives surely didn't actually relax and have fun?

'And by that you mean?'

'We do like to enjoy ourselves too Ruby.'

Aoife tutted, and there was an unusually girly and human-like quality to her that I couldn't quite take in properly.

'I'm talking drinks and dancing. The Unseelie realm has the best clubs you will ever see.'

With that she shoved me towards my room.

After the worst, most confusing, and generally crazy few weeks of my life, I couldn't believe I was getting dressed up for a night out. Aoife and Bran had brought me a load of my possessions from my house earlier on in the week, and I was definitely grateful today as I searched through my party dresses. In the end, I settled for my classic black above-the-knee bodycon dress that was mildly revealing on the chest front. Sadly they had not retrieved my bottle of wine from the fridge so pre-drinks to ease the nerves was not an option.

Putting some music on my phone, I started getting dressed and applying my makeup. For just 20 minutes I felt as though I was back to my normal life. Saffie stayed relatively quiet other than to praise my appearance every now and again. I hummed along to the music, occasionally dancing in front of the mirror.

It's nice to see you actually happy again.

I feel human again.

Be careful tonight.

Are you not coming with me?

Instantly I felt less joyful. I needed Saffie.

No, I've got some leads I want to follow up with.

She paused and then must've noticed the fearful look on my face.

But If you need me I can rearrange.

I wanted desperately to tell her to cancel and come with me, but I knew that we needed to keep our sights on the key aim; to get out of here.

No, its okay, just keep working on getting us out of here. Besides, Aoife will be there and I almost trust her to look after me.

She is a pleasant surprise here.

That was Saffie's way of confirming that she was starting to trust Aoife herself.

A knock on my door had me springing up off the bed, and grinning like the Cheshire cat. I had expected to be opening the door to Aoife, but instead, the Prince stood there. He was dressed in some jeans and a well fitted t-shirt. I had not seen the Prince in such relaxed attire before. My eyes betrayed me as they shamelessly took in every inch of his perfect form.

'Where's Aoife?'

I attempted to keep my tone as cool as possible when

confronted with the most perfect man I had ever seen. No, not man, psychotic Fae prince. I could not lose sight of what they all were.

'We are meeting them down by the castle entrance.'

His smile was cocky.

'So if you're ready human, and finished eyeing me up, then we can head out.'

I gave a sarcastic smile back before saying goodbye to Saffie and exiting the room. Our walk downstairs was, as to be expected, performed in silence. Though I was happy with this, as I had very little to say to the Prince. I was surprised to see at least half of the King's guard standing in the foyer. Most of the group gave disapproving looks as I arrived, but I instantly picked out Oakley and Aoife who were smiling at me. Bran stood there with a forced smile, trying to appease his wife. I instantly gravitated towards them, ignoring the rest of the group who were whispering and sighing at me.

'You look amazing!'

Aoife shot her arms up enthusiastically. I couldn't agree as I stared open mouthed at her. She was beautiful. Her sexy leather look skirt, and low-cut top accentuated every single one of her stunning features. I felt suddenly very incompatible with this group of hyper attractive Unseelie.

Bran opened up a portal in front of us, and a mild sense of trepidation overwhelmed me. I had no idea where we were going, and the idea of using that vomit-inducing portal made me even more nervous.

'Scared?'

The words whispered in my ear. I didn't turn to look, but I could tell the Prince's mocking voice anywhere now. A sense of defiance overcame me and I swallowed down my fear.

'Come on human, let's do this.'

An arm linked through mine and I felt a sense of comfort as Oakley pulled me through the portal.

I'm not sure what I was expecting when we stepped through the portal, but it certainly wasn't the normality I encountered. The street was a variety of closed shops and the odd lit-up bar. I followed, unquestioning, as we entered a lively looking bar. The atmosphere as we entered was intoxicating. Oakley explained briefly to me that the owners had spelled the establishment to be relaxing for those who entered. Apparently this was normal here. We all headed to the bar, as Aoife demanded a round from the barman. Within seconds we were all presented with a line of shots. Normally I would question it, but after the week I had had I couldn't bring myself to care. In sync with the others, I threw back the shot. Within a minute of everyone finishing, another was lined up, and I threw a questioning look to Aoife who simply winked at me.

'Fae are not as vulnerable to alcohol as humans, so do not feel pressured to drink.'

The prince purred in my ear, which I took personally as a challenge, and turned so that he could watch me smugly throw back the next shot. Thankfully, we all ordered proper drinks after that one as I was not as confident as I had pretended to be.

As I sipped on my Sauvignon I leaned against the bar and actually started to take in my surroundings. The place was of course full of Fae. I was shocked to see how many different races of Fae existed. The Unseelie were definitely the most human-looking. The only similarity I could visibly see between them all was that they were all insanely beautiful. Even those with a peculiar green shimmer to their skin.

I suddenly felt like the ugly duckling as I took in the sea of beautiful creatures ahead of me.

'You look like you could use another drink.'

A voice next to me took me by surprise, and I span around to see Farrell, one of the king's guard. I eyed him curiously for a minute, he had never been pleasant before to me, so I was half waiting for the sarcastic joke to follow. But It didn't. Instead, he gave me a reassuring smile and went ahead and ordered me another wine and a shot of something that I didn't quite catch the name of.

'Cheers!'

He held his shot glass up, and so I followed suit and clinked mine against his before drinking it. The shot burnt my throat as it went down, and left me coughing embarrassingly afterwards.

'What the hell was that? It was vile!'

'A Seelie slammer.'

He grinned mischievously before leaning and whispering in my ear.

'You looked like you needed to relax a bit, you can thank me later.'

Before I could question him, he sauntered back off into the crowd. Great. I decided to take it easy and make that glass of wine last a while, until I could determine how strongly that shot would affect me. Farrall had appeared cheeky, as though he was pulling a prank on me, but not harmful so that put my mind at rest a little.

'Come dance!'

Aoife came pushing through the crowd, a ridiculously big smile on her face, and grabbed my arm to pull me through to where a bunch of them were merrily dancing. I noticed the Prince wasn't with them, but didn't bother to ask his whereabouts because it seemed likely he was off being moody and sultry at the bar somewhere. I began to feel a light warmth through me before my head started to get a little giddy. I started to feel more relaxed and free as I actually laughed with the group of Unseelie and danced playfully with them. The fears and stresses seemed to melt away, and in that moment, I decided that I indeed would have to thank Farrell later. I'm not sure at what point the prince joined us but one minute I closed my eyes as I swayed my hips to the music, and the next I opened them and he was there with us. To my surprise there was a little two-step type movement as well, and a genuine smile on his face as he laughed with Bran. This new chilled side of him was incredibly sexy. Wait, was that actually what I thought? There was a different kind of heat that I was noticing now going on.

'Aoife, what's in a Seelie Slammer?'

I grabbed Aoife so I could whisper in her ear.

'Oh god you don't want one of those, your human body would be in a drunk sensory overload!'

She must have noticed the horrified look on my face.

'Great, who gave you one?'

'Farrell.'

"Right, I will deal with him later. Just, try to relax."

She laughed shaking her head. Well if she was laughing then that had to mean I was in no danger, just seemingly a bit more frisky than normal.

I was enthusiastically dancing and singing along with the music when I noticed a figure lurking beside me. I turned, only to be stunned as a gorgeous man held out a drink for me, and displayed a warm sexy smile. It may have been the 'Seelie slammer' but I felt every part of me flush warm and I couldn't help the girly smile and giggle that came out in response.

'Don't worry it's not drugged, your friend over there watched.'

He laughed as held the drink to me and I hesitated. Like a schoolgirl, I just managed to giggle and take the drink gratefully. His bright blue eyes were captivating, and images of running my hands through his blonde cropped hair overwhelmed my brain. His figure was like a rugby player, and I felt myself going giddy as I imagined those big strong biceps folding around me. I was certain I was staring, and possibly drooling, but his warm smile never faltered. Instead, he held a hand out and winked, suggesting a dance. I wanted to throw myself on him, but settled for taking his hand, attempting to not seem as ridiculously keen as I was.

ASH

I watched in disgust as Adriel slimed up to Ruby and presented her with another alcoholic drink. It was rare for me to hold such a low opinion of an Unseelie, but he was one of those rarities. He was exuding his natural charm that seemed to easily woo women, particularly human women. He was the type of male that I couldn't stand, he found humans easy pickings and took great pleasure in making his way into the pants of any remotely attractive one he came across. It was particularly distasteful for a Fae to have such interactions with humans. I had hoped that Ruby would be sensible enough to resist his persuasive and perfected smile, but based on the glow to her cheeks and the ridiculous shifting on the spot she was doing, I could see that she was as gullible as the rest. Whilst it was not a crime to bed humans, the Unseelie who did so were generally regarded with a certain degree of disgust by those with more self-respect. I glanced at Aoife, hoping that she had witnessed the events unfolding, and would be keen to intervene. However, she was dancing with Bran and didn't seem to notice. I continued to observe subtly, anger starting to bubble as I watched him pull her towards him and start to run his hands down her delicate but curvy figure. I waited, hoping that she would display some refusal that would justify me going over and stopping him, but she didn't. Her body moved in time with his, and a sexy smile spread across her face in pleasure at his attention. This was an embarrassment for us. The King's guard was a pillar of strength and organisation to all, and this little demonstration would do no good for our reputation.

'Ooh the newest recruit is a hit already.'

Aoife pranced over to me. I raised my eyebrow at her, unable to understand why she didn't feel concerned by the situation.

'I thought you liked the human?'

'I do. She is just dancing.'

'With Adriel. She's going to make a fool of herself and the King's guard by being another human conquest.'

'Look around, no-one else is going to even entertain polite chitchat with her, at least this way she receives some positive attention and can feel less like the odd one out. I'm watching her, I just feel she will benefit from some down-time. Besides, she's just dancing off the Seelie slammer, if she were completely human she'd be getting naked and humping his leg by now.'

She almost doubled over in laughter at the idea. My blood instantly boiled. Who in Fae hell had played that prank on her? I knew that I shouldn't be so mad, the other guards had no idea of the magnitude of the situation.

'Who gave her the drink?'

I couldn't hide the fury behind my words, and Aoife's face instantly sobered. She hesitated about answering, but my glare had her spilling quickly

'Farrall.'

She recoiled as a low growl escaped my chest. My eyes darted back to Ruby, who was grinding her hips beneath Adriel's hands, and his lecherous eyes were roaming all over her.

There was only so much that I could take, and against Aoife's advice I made my way over and gently touched Ruby's arm to alert her of my presence. She turned her head and looked me straight in the eyes, her intoxicated brain taking longer to process everything. I indicated to her with a head tilt, and she reluctantly tore herself from Adriel, whispering in his ear quickly before following me to the bar.

'What's up?'

There was an aroused flush to her cheeks, and her eyes darted back to Adriel briefly. I took a minute to calm my irritation before answering. The girl was technically a victim. Why she would accept a drink from those who clearly did not like her was beyond me. It confirmed what I already knew; humans were simple creatures.

'I've been made aware that you were given a 'Seelie slammer', I don't know what you know about the drink but it's not suitable for human consumption.'

I managed to keep my voice level, despite being acutely aware that she was only half listening.

'So I've been told, but I feel fine actually.'

She gave a half-hearted smile, clearly keen to return to her previous antics. I raised an eyebrow at her and glanced over towards the dance floor, pointedly.

'The way you were behaving over there suggested otherwise.'

Suddenly her eyebrows shot up, and her attention was completely focussed on our conversation.

'And what exactly was my behaviour over there?'

Her tone held a hint of warning, as if I were overstepping a boundary. I felt speechless for a moment. This was not the reaction that I had expected.

'You were not acting yourself was what I meant.'

I attempted a more diplomatic approach, to play it safe in public, though this didn't seem to appease her either.

'Myself? You seem to forget that you have no idea who I am. The 'me' that you have seen and claim to know is a prisoner, nothing more.'

I had wanted to argue back, but her words rang too truthful to argue with. Saving me from any further uncomfortable conflict, Aoife squeezed in between us and announced that we would be moving onto another bar. The temptation to down a line of shots before we left was there, but knowing the hell my father would unleash tomorrow held me back. Instead, I followed behind the group as they made their way through the town to a variety of bars over the course of the evening. Whilst they partied and released all tension from their minds, I remained sober with my couple of drinks per place visited, and I was reminded exactly why I didn't bother to entertain evenings out anymore. The only bright side was that we did not have the misfortune of running into Adriel again, and the rest of the evening remained relatively tame.

CHAPTER SIX

RUBY

Groaning, I peeled open my dried-out eyes. Saffie was sitting next to me, staring and looking unimpressed.

Don't give me that look Saf, the hangover from hell is judgment enough.

No judgment here Ruby, I am just hoping you will clean that pool of sick up soon, as the smell is pretty offensive.

I strained my neck to peer over the edge of the bed, and sure enough just before the door to the en-suite was a puddle of puke. Lovely. My phone beeped and I decided to drag the duvet over my head instead of looking at it. It could only have been minutes after the message alert that my room was burst into.

'Get up, did you not see my message?'

Aoife's voice was authoritative and firm. When I didn't respond, I heard her light steps come across the room and before I knew it the duvet was ripped away from me. I scowled up at her, and her stern face faltered slightly as she tried not to laugh at me.

'You look awful.'

'Thanks, Aoife. Can always trust Fae to make you feel better eh?'

'You have 5 minutes to get up and make yourself presentable.'

Her eyes roamed over towards the bathroom.

'And clean that up, the smell is foul.'

With that she spun on her heel and exited the room, closing the door behind her. I ignored Saffie's 'I told you so' look that she was throwing me whilst I dragged my lifeless body up out of bed.

Perhaps I should have gone with you last night.

Amusement was evident in her tone. I did not appreciate that.

Well, I can safely say I have also learned that in addition to my many other failures among the Fae, I also fail at keeping up with their drinking abilities.

My stomach churned threateningly and so I tried to move slowly to prevent the risk of any further vomiting incidents.

Care to elaborate on last night's events?

Later, I don't want to think about it right now. Even the thought of alcohol right now...

I paused that thought as an audible retching escaped my throat. Clamping my hand over my mouth and taking breaths through my nose I managed to stop any repeats. I heard Saffie's chuckle in my head and simply threw a glare in her direction.

'I don't know if I can do this.'

I groaned as I hovered some tissue above the vomit pile.

Well, you better had, because you are not leaving it there.

Saffie warned, her face slightly scrunched in disgust. Muttering under my breath and swallowing down my near-repeat offenses, I managed to clear it up fairly speedily.

Having thrown on some fresh clothes, thrown my hair back and over sprayed myself with body spray, I made my way down towards the breakfast hall. The king's guard all ate together in the mornings and discussed the plan for the day and all notifications, I guess like a team building sort of routine. I was evidently late as everyone turned to stare at me skulking in, Saffie in tow and appearing embarrassed. Oakley nodded his head to the seat he had saved for me, next to him. Shooting him my best grateful look I silently sped over and sat down. I could only hope and pray that my stomach was not actually audible in its tantrum against last night's alcohol.

'Now that Ruby has finally graced us with her presence, we can get started.'

The Prince shot me a disapproving look, and I immediately dropped my eyes to the full plate of pastry and fruit in front of me. Embarrassment was most definitely not what I needed at this stage. Saffie hopped gracefully onto my lap, and more dirty looks shot my way. Some of the Unseelie guards had previously announced their disgust toward my feline friend sitting at the table with us, but thankfully the familiar role trumped their pathetic cat hatred. I had asked Saffie previously why there were no other familiars around the castle. She explained that not everyone had a familiar, and there was no real understanding of why some supernaturals would have one and others wouldn't. I had no idea why I had been blessed with one, but I would just be forever grateful that I was. Saffie had also told me that she had no interest in interacting with the other familiars. She was as keen to leave the Fae realm as I was. Since then Saffie had been pretty smug about being at the table and liked to look each guard in the eyes that had opposed her presence. It was easy to see why we got on so well. Everyone commenced eating whilst the prince rambled on about Unseelie politics and other things that I couldn't have cared less about. A gentle claw to the leg made my head snap up and Saffie inclined her head to the prince, indicating I needed to listen.

'As you can imagine, if he is not apprehended then there will be further severe risks for both the Fae realm and the human world. Viktor is not just an ordinary vampire, he appears to have plans that we are not yet fully aware of, but are likely to be catastrophic. He has no fear of repercussions and has a lot of power, added to that he obviously has help otherwise his escape would never have been possible.'

I felt my blood run cold. Viktor was free. That wink after the court case had been an indication that he knew he would get away. The urge to be sick again rushed over me, and I grabbed the edge of my seat as I fought it back down. Saffie grumbled to herself and her eyes darted around the room as if suddenly suspicious of everyone in it. I glanced up at Aoife, but she was engrossed and animated in her planning with the Prince and Bran. Everyone else appeared relatively unaffected as they continued their idle chat over the breakfast.

Saf I have a seriously bad feeling about this. He winked at me as he left the court room. He knew he would get out, and the look he gave me suggested I wouldn't fare as well this time.

I nervously stared at Saffie, and her worried look back showed she had thought similarly.

I won't let him hurt you, Ruby. We need to find him before he finds you and carries out whatever plans he has.

I nodded to her in agreement. My nauseous feeling had increased tenfold now.

After breakfast, everybody filed out of the hall and separated into their ordered groups for the assignments. Oakley, Gerard, Sophie, and I had been tasked with searching the castle and the grounds. I had tried to convince Aoife to let me go with her, Bran, and the Prince to the human realm but I was ignored. Supposedly they had allies in the human world who they needed to talk to, in case Viktor had returned there. Orders were to apprehend Viktor by whatever means necessary, and only to kill him as a last resort. The thought of having to fight and potentially kill someone, even a vampire who destroyed my life, filled me with even more nausea and dread.

'Don't worry, the chances of him being anywhere near this castle now are so slim.'

Oakley smiled in an attempt to reassure me. It didn't.

'Of course he won't be here, the Prince just needed people to babysit the human and make her feel important.'

Sophie tutted, looking more than a little annoyed. Gerard sniggered at her remark.

'Don't start Sophie.'

Oakley threw me an apologetic glance.

'Why don't we split up and search, that way we can cover our ground quicker and get more time off before the evening training session.'

His suggestion did prove Sophie's comment to be true, but I was grateful for him removing the animosity aimed at me. Sophie and Gerard agreed and claimed the indoors as their search territory, so Oakley and I made our way outdoors to search in the snowy castle gardens.

'Thank you for that back there Oakley.'

I smiled genuinely at him. Whilst I had come to see

Aoife as a close friend here, and in fact my first friend here, Oakley had quickly become one of my favourite Unseelie. Unlike the others, he didn't seem to have the same sarcastic, hot, and cold attitude. When he smiled it was genuine and heartfelt, and he had been one of the only ones to never outwardly mock or judge me.

'You're very different to the others in the king's guard.'

The words came out before I realised that I could have sounded insulting. Thankfully he just smiled.

'That's because I am.'

He pointed towards the South Gardens as our first area to head towards, before continuing.

'My father was Unseelie, and my mother was Nymph. It was challenging to say the least at first, to fit in with the Unseelie court, I had to prove that I was not weaker than the rest of them.'

Immediately it made sense, he was kind to me because he knew how I felt

'Don't get me wrong, I was in higher standing than you as I was at least fully Fae, but I do know what it's like to have to prove yourself. You will get there Ruby, your Fae strength and determination will come through for you.'

Making our way through the gardens I couldn't help but be enthralled by its beauty, and despite the freezing temperatures I was thriving off the fresh air. This was my first time venturing out into the castle grounds since I had arrived, and the view from my room had shown me that the gardens were beautiful, but in person, they were so much more. For all of my hatred towards my prison, I had to admit that I was starting to appreciate the true beauty of it too. Cold and harsh, but also the most naturally stunning creation I had ever seen. We made our way through the wooden archway that was laced with vines and white roses. Throughout the first garden was a multitude of colourful flowers that I had never seen before. I could only smile at the gorgeous aroma as we passed through.

'What are they?'

I gasped as I saw tiny little things zip past my face and into the flowers.

'I would be careful not to offend them, they are sprites, they tend to the gardens and are very fiery towards those who do not offer them respect.'

Oakley raised his eyebrows at me in a warning. I gulped and then returned my gaze to the sprites, watching them work carefully but thoroughly. Incredible. One seemed to notice us and flew straight up to Oakley, suspicion on her little face. She was very much a tiny figurine-sized version of the Unseelie; perfect looks, a serious face, and pointed ears.

'Can I help you?'

'Yes, we are looking for a vampire named Viktor. He is wanted by the court and has fled, have you seen him?'

The sprite's face flashed shock and then went neutral before she took on a managerial tone and called over some other sprites to confirm that no vampires had been seen. We thanked her and moved on through the garden to head to the next.

'So, what brought you into the King's guard then if you knew that you would be looked down upon from the start?'

I hoped that he wouldn't consider me intrusive. One thing I had learned about the Fae was that they were pretty reserved and secretive.

'Well...'

He paused and seemed to consider his answer carefully before continuing

'When I was young my father was killed in battle whilst

serving the realm, and from that point on I had a clear vision in my mind for my future. My father was very loyal to the throne and I wanted to continue in his footsteps and mission.'

His face had become quite serious and almost angry as he seemed to reflect.

'I'm so sorry that you had to experience that, it must have been awful.'

I gently touched his arm in a supportive gesture, but this appeared to bring him back to the present and his serious expression was instantly replaced with a relaxed smile once again. An uneasy feeling washed through me. His ability to switch off his emotions in such a way was a strong reminder of our fundamental differences.

'That was a long time ago, and I am pretty certain he would be pleased with how I have since conducted my life and work.'

His grin spread and I couldn't help but smile in response.

'Enough about me though, tell me about your human life. I'm intrigued to know who Ruby is back in her own world.'

I wanted to ask more about his family, but his diversion from the topic made it abundantly clear that he was done with the subject.

ASH

Having distributed groups of the King's guard over the realm to search for Viktor, I had decided to involve the human allies to aid us in capturing him. Assuming that Viktor was likely long gone from the castle grounds, I had decided to put Ruby in the group checking those surroundings. It had seemed like the best option for someone who could prove more of a hindrance than a help in actual combat. Plus that frustrating little voice in my head had urged me to put her in the safest position available. Aoife, Bran, and I made our way through a portal and to the supernatural council in the human world. We arrived at the building and though a few people were briefly startled, they quickly resumed their work and tried to not look directly at us. The premises was cloaked with a spell so that only employees and supernaturals could see it for what it was. To the unsuspecting humans, it was simply a run-down office building in the city, nothing out of the ordinary or noticeable. However, inside the cloak, it was a heavily manned, high-tech resource centre for the humans to monitor the effects of the supernaturals. The Unseelie had come to an agreement with the humans around 100 years ago to work together to ensure that the supernatural world was kept a secret and to minimise the effects that they had on the humans. It was a mutually beneficial but strained relationship that had lasted surprisingly well.

Heading in, we were greeted by David Chambers immediately and taken straight over to the overly large wall-mounted screen that had Viktor's face displayed on it. David was a tall and slender human, with the stereotypical 'geek' look that one would expect to work in a place like this. I was able to just about tolerate him in short bursts.

'We haven't had any reports in the last week, but there have been some interesting links and patterns established prior to his capture. He appears to have been methodical in where he went, and who he killed.'

David's voice shook ever so slightly. He was still uncomfortable in our presence, but he maintained his focus. I preferred it this way, these humans needed to be conscious that they were replaceable. Humans, as a species, are known to be greedy and self-serving creatures. If we did not keep them in check here then they would, without a doubt, become a risk to the operation. That was a mess that I did not have the time to clean up. He motioned to a colleague who tapped away on the computer and changed the screen display to a map with four red location dots on it.

'It appears he targeted a witch coven in North London about a month ago, and that was where the pattern started initially-from what we know. He killed them all and trashed their home seemingly trying to find something.'

'What was he looking for?'

'We have no idea, but he was determined that's for sure. From there, he moved on to another coven, and the same happened again. Although this time we feel he may have found something more worthwhile.'

'Why do you think that?'

'Because the coven held 6 witches, and only 5 bodies were found.'

'He took a witch?'

Aoife's voice showed her surprise. David nodded his assumption.

'It didn't end there though, he made his way through two other covens and from what we can tell took a variety of items specific to those covens.'

It was not adding up. There were too many pieces that did not fit together. This was not the work of one lone vampire, that much I felt certain of.

'Any news on accomplices? There has to be more than just him. There is no way he has successfully slaughtered four witch covens and lived to tell the tale. Keep us informed if you find out anything more, we are searching the Fae realm, but he will likely return here.'

David nodded obediently, beads of sweat forming on his forehead.

'We should add a tag for the bar he hit on the night he attacked Ruby, it may be relevant.'

Bran suggested.

'Ruby?'

David's meek voice tremored, trying to engage in the conversation. We did not acknowledge him and he quickly got the hint to stand quietly until he was directly spoken to.

'Are we considering that more than just an easy feeding opportunity now then?'

Aoife stood with one hand on her hip, her brow creasing as she too tried to connect the dots.

'Bran is right, we need to consider everything to be calculated at this point, there is more to this vampire than we realised.'

I responded, my frown deepening as I considered the endless possibilities. Bran gave the location to the brunette lady who was furiously tapping away on her computer as if her life depended on it. I could practically hear her heart pounding against her ribcage and her raspy rapid breathing as Bran leaned over the desk next to her. Presumably, she was feeling a mixture of arousal and complete terror. We seemed to have that effect on the humans.

Bran broke the silence as we returned to the lobby.

'This is bad. If he is targeting witches in the human realm and Unseelie in the Fae realm, he wants power and that is something that a vampire has little use for.'

'My thoughts exactly Bran, Viktor is the errand boy.'

The words span around my head as I said them

'But if he is working for someone, and we are considering the possibility that Ruby was actually targeted then that would indicate that someone considerably worse has plans for her.'

'We need to return to the castle.'

I felt immensely uncomfortable at our lack of knowledge of the situation. There was no possible way that I could prepare for something when I had no idea what I was dealing with. Aoife prepared a portal and we silently made our way through, all of us lost in our thoughts over the mysterious bigger player.

CHAPTER SEVEN

RUBY

Having returned to my room after a fruitless endeavour to find our missing captive, I settled for a lazy couple of hours lying on my bed and replying to group messages with my friends. Mostly it was discussions over how irritating their husbands were for not helping out, and how Carly's kids were little nightmares. The last message was Faye organising her engagement party. As a bridesmaid, and one of her closest friends, I was of course assumed to be attending. How would I explain that I have been abducted by fairies and now have joined a fairy security team to capture an evil vampire? They would either think I'd lost it completely, or that I was willing to say anything to not go. I would have to try to find a way of going to the party, perhaps an Aoife-shaped chaperone might convince the prince that I wouldn't become the next escapee. Or perhaps Oakley would be a more fitting choice. Next to me Saffie stretched out, and yawned, clearly enjoying the comfortable luxuries we currently had.

Don't get too used to this lifestyle Saff, we will be going home at some point.

She ignored me and made her way out of the cat flap that she had demanded be installed in our bedroom door.

'Bye then!'

She paused briefly before exiting to turn and look at me.

I'm going to get some lunch and fresh air; I will be back in time for training.

'You're so grumpy when you first wake up.'

She gave me her classic deadpan stare before continuing out of the cat flap. Sassy kitty.

A knock on the door startled me and broke me out of my sleepy daze. I reluctantly beckoned them to enter. I groaned as to my surprise, the Prince opened the door and walked in. He glanced me up and down disapprovingly for a minute before commenting.

'Judging by your relaxed state, I take it there was nothing to report from your search?'

He was clearly not impressed, but there was something else in his face that I couldn't quite determine.

'No. I assumed you wouldn't mind me being out of the way, saves the others from having to babysit me and waste their time.'

I raised my eyebrow at him, half hoping that he would deny my claim and make me feel just a fraction less useless. But that would not be the Unseelie way.

'Never hurts to double-check an area, and keep the weak link feeling busy and useful.'

The humour in his voice was audible.

'Wow! So, did you come here just to mock me, or can I help you with something?'

'I actually do need to ask you some questions.'

His face returned to serious.

'The night that Viktor drank from you at the club, did you see anyone else with him at any point?'

I shook my head in response.

'I need to be sure, I need all of the details, even ones you don't realise you saw.'

'If I don't know that I saw something, how can I tell you?'

'I need to search your mind.'

'No. Absolutely not. No more mind play. I still get headaches from those creepy bastards that mentally annihilated me!'

A violent shiver ran down my spine at the memory of being tortured by the Fae elders.

'This isn't the same Ruby, it's not painful.'

He took in my reluctance before adding.

'It is also not optional.'

He took a seat on the edge of my bed, an action which stirred an unusual feeling In my stomach, and held his hands out to me. I hesitantly nodded and took his hands. A tingling sensation went through me and I had to cough gently and look down in the hope that he didn't notice the blush spreading across my cheeks. Why the hell was I reacting like this?

'Relax.'

His deep, sexy voice instructed. Sexy? Stop it brain.

'I need you to think back to that evening, and replay it all. You will feel me trying to get inside your mind, just let me in.'

I stifled a girly giggle. What the hell was wrong with me?

Clearing my throat, I pushed any naughty thoughts to

the back of my mind, acutely aware that he may otherwise hear them shortly. I closed my eyes and thought back to being picked up in the car with the girls to go out. I felt a warming presence pushing slightly in my head, and assuming that was the Prince, I relaxed and let the presence watch over me. I was at the bar collecting the shots, when I heard the Prince's voice.

Take it slowly Ruby, I need to see who was around you.

I slowed down and started to take in faces around me, the barman was the most clear as I had been trying to get his attention for drinks. There were lots of people at the bar though, some faces were blurry and some were relatively clear.

There, to your right. I recognise that face from somewhere.

I whipped my head to the right again, trying to work out who he meant. I hesitated for a moment before he instructed that I continue the memory.

You look very happy with your friends.

That's because I was. It wasn't a perfect or exciting life I had before all of this, but it was mine. My friends may just be simple humans to you, but they have more loyalty and love in them than any of you lot would know what to do with.

He went quiet again after my response, so I continued my memory. When it got to the point of seeing Viktor on the dance floor, I felt a wave of anger wash over me that I was certain wasn't mine, considering I was nothing but enthralled and turned on at the time of meeting him. Now I was of course disgusted at my hormones, but I couldn't blame my naïve former self for not having expected a vampire of all things. As soon as we got outside and he started kissing me, I felt the mental connection drop and blinked open my eyes to find the Prince had dropped my hands.

'Thank you Ruby that was very helpful.'

With that, he swiftly got up and exited my room. My head was still spinning from the memory tap, but even in my slightly confused state, I could tell that something was wrong with the Prince.

That was odd.

I heard Saffie's voice from across the room.

'Saff? When did you get back?'

About ten minutes ago. What the hell was all that about?

ASH

I escaped Ruby's room speedily, worried that the tremor in my hands would have been noticeable. Memories were tricky things to delve into. It was a rare and dangerous skill, one that I had been careful not to overuse since my near miss. If I had overstepped the line by even a fraction too much then I would have been trapped in the prison of my own mind. The shaking would wear off soon enough, and it was worth it to obtain the information that we would have otherwise not had access to. Clasping my hands behind my back, I approached Bran who had been wandering the hallway.

'Bran, my study in twenty minutes.'

Bran silently nodded and carried on his way. Taking a deep breath, I marched to my father's chambers. I only managed a single knock before his deep voice summoned me in.

'Your Highness.'

I gave a brief bow before approaching him. At his desk

he looked almost aged with his brow creased, his eyes didn't leave the maps of the realm strewn in front of him.

'I'm assuming that as you have interrupted me, you have some important updates on the whereabouts of our missing captive?'

'I visited the human world to determine what had been established there regarding Viktor's movements, and whilst they haven't had any recent encounters, they did manage to stumble across a very interesting pattern prior to his capture.'

This earned me a glance up from his otherwise important business. He nodded for me to continue.

'Viktor and his accomplices slaughtered witch covens in search of some presumably rare and powerful items, he also took one witch that we had only assumed to be a hostage.'

'Assumed?'

My father raised his eyebrow at me.

'We assumed hostage based on the evidence, that is until I visited our guest Ruby Goodall to confirm details about her encounter with Viktor. When searching her memories, I was surprised to see a face that I hadn't in a long while; Katherine Sparrow. She was in the bar on the night when Viktor attacked Ruby, and from what I could see she did not resemble much of a hostage.'

His frown deepened, and for a moment I considered that he may have been showing apprehension over my use of dangerous magic. I quickly quashed that notion.

'You're sure that is the witch he took?'

His focus remained solely on the job at hand.

'No, but I intend to find out.'

'See that you do, I want him and his accomplices apprehended swiftly. What of Miss Goodall? Any development?'

'She has improved in her training, but there is little else to report currently.'

'Then push harder, there is something more to her.'

'Yes, sire.'

With that, I exited his chambers and made my way to my office in preparation for the meeting with Bran.

'Come in Bran.'

I called as I heard his tentative knock on my door. He entered, face tight and prepared for negative news.

'It would appear the witch Katherine Sparrow may be involved with Viktor.'

'Katherine? Last I heard she was settled in a coven in the human realm...'

His voice trailed off as he started to make the same connection that I had.

'You think she was the missing witch from the slaughtered coven? But what makes you think that?'

'She was in the bar on the night Viktor attacked Ruby, which further confirms the suspicion that it was not a coincidence that Ruby was targeted.'

'But why would Katherine help a vampire? Witches and vampires are hardly friendly with one another.'

'I don't know. But if a witch is actively involved then that would explain how they pulled off the collection of magical items from a variety of covens. We need to investigate the coven where the witch went missing, we need to know if it indeed is Katherine and how she is involved. Get yourself, Aoife, and Ruby ready to leave in thirty minutes. I also want the other attacked covens to be inspected thoroughly, we need to know what has been taken if we are to get an idea of what they are planning.'

'You want Ruby to come with us?'

Bran's confusion was plastered across his face. My gut

instinct was telling me to bring her with us, and it had never been wrong before. Besides, she was less likely to get herself into trouble if she remained under my watch. Regardless of my reasoning, Bran was not in a position to question my decision. I raised my brow at Bran, inviting him to push the matter. Wisely, he chose to nod obediently and exit to assemble to guards.

RUBY

Despite being unsure of why I had been grouped with the big bosses of the king's guard, I complied with the orders and accepted that Saffie was not welcome on this surprise outing. Saffie gave Bran a filthy look and some choice words when he informed us that she would not be attending, but he seemed completely unfazed and disinterested in her protests. Aoife had tried to smooth the situation over by explaining that we were entering the human world and Saffie would not contribute to an inconspicuous look. As I made my way down to the castle entrance, Aoife met me with a cheerful smile and a couple of small knives.

'You know it's considered creepy to come at someone with a knife like that.'

'Oh Ruby, if I planned to kill you then you wouldn't even see me or the knife coming, let alone my smile.'

Then she cackled at her own joke. It would take some more time for me to get used to the Unseelie sense of humour, but I nervously smiled along.

'But these are actually for you to take, just in case.'

'In case of what?'

'In case we run into anyone whom you may need to use them against.'

Ever the cryptic Unseelie response, as I should have expected. I took the two knives and tucked them into the belt she also handed me.

The Prince and Bran stood by the castle entrance, faces serious as they conversed presumably about what we were going into. They turned to look at us as we approached, Bran warmed gently at Aoife and I was surprised to see the Prince relax his features. Naturally, my cheeks blushed as my irritatingly human body responses betrayed my wish to 'play it cool'. That appeared to bring forth a cocky smirk to his face as he stared into my eyes, which just irritated me more. Thankfully Bran broke the unusual eye contact between the Prince and me by offering to prepare the portal. The prince nodded silently and led the way outside. Aoife eyed me curiously for a moment before filing out also. Bran dutifully offered to enter the portal first, as a line of protection on the other side for the Prince. Aoife hesitated, clearly expecting to chaperone me through, but interestingly the Prince gave her a look and nod indicating for her to go through next. After Aoife had stepped through, I sucked in a deep breath and closed my eyes ready to step forward, however, a hand gripped around my arm and stopped me from moving forward. I opened my eyes to see the Prince holding my arm, a conflicted look on his face

'We are going to attend where a coven was slaughtered by Viktor, I highly doubt he will be there but it's vital that you keep your wits about you and be prepared for any surprises.'

His voice hinted that he was concerned and his long fingers gripping my arm sent unexpected feelings through me. It was almost as if he were being protective of me, but the minute I began to question it he dropped his hand and resumed his stern expression to nod me through the portal.

I stepped through and was shocked to be greeted with what resembled a horror movie scene. I couldn't say what I would have expected, but the blood painted on the walls, floors, and most surfaces was not it. It had clearly been a nice and well-furnished home prior to whatever devastation had occurred. A large broken canvas lay on the floor, propped slightly against the wall. It showed several women of varying ages, presumably the witches in this coven. I felt my stomach churn, threatening to bring up the lunch I had scoffed in my room previously. Aoife gravitated to my side, giving me a look that I would guess she had intended to be reassuring.

'Where are the bodies?'

My voice came out like a mouse's squeak.

'Other witches will have taken them to give them a respectful burial.'

Aoife answered as she began to explore the room. How they all looked so unaffected by the scene around us was baffling me.

'Aoife, Bran, take the upstairs. Ruby and I will search down here.'

The Prince commanded. I stood awkwardly for a moment whilst the others went up the stairs. What on earth was I meant to be doing? It appeared the team had forgotten this was my first outing in the King's guard, let alone my first crime scene investigation.

'Erm, excuse me?'

The Prince turned and gave me a confused look.

'What am I supposed to be doing?'

That blush crept back over my face as I felt like a complete moron under his gaze.

'We are looking for indications of a witch called

Katherine Sparrow residing here, and any clues of missing magical items that Viktor may have taken.'

The Unseelie's ability to make me feel ridiculously small and stupid was starting to get on my nerves, and I felt my temper starting to flare a bit.

'Right... so what am I supposed to do? I don't know who this Katherine is, and I have no idea how to search for magical items, currently the most I'm managing to do is force my lunch to stay down in this horrific setting.'

My sarcasm was definitely evident in my tone, and as soon as I had finished, I wondered if I would regret being disrespectful to the Unseelie Prince. To my surprise, he looked mildly amused, which just frustrated me more. He was about to respond when the sound of crashing behind me made me scream and fling myself forward towards him. He caught me, and we both looked around to see Bran at the bottom of the stairs. He swiftly jumped to his feet again and shot back up the stairs shouting to us.

'Vampires!"

The Prince spun me behind him just in time as three vampires burst through the front door and aimed straight for us. My heart pounded so hard I was sure everyone could hear it, and the threat of vomiting became even more pronounced.

'Get back Ruby!'

The Prince yelled as he retracted his small sword and began swinging it at the vampires. I stumbled backward, in a state of shock. This was nothing like training. One of the vampires threw himself at the Prince, dodging an attempted blow from the sword. The Prince managed to deliver a quick return swing but only clipped the shoulder in passing. It grabbed at his clothing and tried to drag him closer. The

Prince retaliated with a hard elbow to the face. The Vampire stumbled backwards momentarily but by this time the other two had engaged and the Prince was desperately trying to fend them off. Remembering I had my knives, I quickly extracted them from my belt and held them pathetically In front of me. One of the vampires seemed to then notice me, ducked the Prince's sword swing, and darted towards me. I tried to stab one of the knives forward but he was far too quick and even gave me an evil grin as he sidestepped it.

'You must be the human half-breed.'

He hissed through his fangs. I swung the knife at him, hoping to slash his belly, but again he stepped backward and I missed. He took my miss as an opportunity to lunge forward and grab me. I felt my body crash into the wall with a crunching thud, as he pressed against me he whispered in my ear

'I heard you taste divine.'

With that, my body finally reacted for me, my hands pushed back and shoved him hard enough that he stumbled backward. From the corner of my eye, I saw the prince decapitate the last of the two he was fighting. My hands shot out in front of me and before I knew what was happening an orange pulse shot from them, setting my attacker alight. He released a piercing screech as the flames ate away at him with supernatural speed. Within seconds he had fallen silent and crumbled to the ground in a pile of ash.

My palms felt hot, and my eyes shot back and forth, from the ash pile to my hands. What the hell had just happened? Did I just set a vampire on fire with my hands?!

'Ruby.'

The Prince's voice snapped me out of my meltdown spiral, but I had no response. I searched his eyes for some sort of reassurance, but instead was met with caution and what looked like worry. Noticing my fear, he softened his look and gently moved forward extending his hands out to me. When I didn't move or respond, he delicately placed his hands on mine and lowered them for me.

'Are you okay?'

'No.'

My voice came out a barely audible squeak before tears rolled down my cheeks and I fought desperately to stop the hysterical crying from breaking through. The Prince's hand let go of mine and instead moved to brush my hair from their sweat-soaked position stuck to my cheeks. Instinctively I wrapped my arms around him and began to cry, more shockingly he embraced me back and stood quietly hugging me for a moment. Aoife and Bran appeared at the bottom of the stairs, faces unreadable at what they were witnessing.

'Have you finished upstairs?'

The Prince asked sounding defensive, but not releasing me.

'Y-yes, the vampires are dead and we found evidence of Katherine's presence in the coven.'

Bran stammered.

'Good, head back to the castle.'

'But...'

Bran's protest was cut off instantly as I can only assume the Prince gave him the 'don't question me' look. Aoife gave me one more concerned look before she and Bran disappeared through a portal.

I was the first to pull away from the embrace.

'What just happened?' I asked, my brain completely incapable of making sense of it all

'I will explain it to you soon Ruby, but for now, I need you to promise me that you will not tell anyone about this.'

His voice was suddenly so serious and anxious that I felt my fear building again.

'Why?'

'Please just trust me, I will explain it when I can, but if anyone finds out about that then you will be in grave danger. I need to figure out what it all means.'

I managed a nod of agreement before he created a portal and pulled me through it.

CHAPTER EIGHT

RUBY

My mind was racing as I entered my bedroom. Saffie stretched out on the bed and yawned as my arrival awoke her.

Fun mission?

She asked before she paused, taking in my appearance.

Ruby, what's wrong? What happened?

I opened my mouth to respond but instead just found myself tearing up, throwing myself onto the bed, and burying my head in the pillow. Saffie nuzzled my arm before curling up beside me and silently comforting me. Whilst Saff and I hadn't technically known each other long, it was as though our souls had known each other forever. She knew how to handle me, how to comfort and support me. She had become as vital to me as one of my organs, and no matter what happened I could only be grateful for her coming into my life and weathering this crazy storm with me.

At least an hour must have passed before I finally rolled my head to look at Saffie and tell her what had happened.

That can't be. Ruby, that sort of power is not possible for normal Fae, let alone half-breeds like you. What you've described is fire magic.

Fire magic? What the hell is fire magic?

It's a type of magic that draws from the sun, but that sort of magic is only accessed by the most powerful of Fae, there are only certain bloodlines that have access to that elemental magic. This just isn't possible.

Saff, I really don't understand a damn word you're saying.

I tried not to get frustrated, but she was clearly forgetting that she was speaking to a mere human with no supernatural insight. Her voice became more stern.

Think about what I am saying Ruby. If only certain bloodlines of strong Fae have access to an elemental magic, and you have accessed it...

Then I belong to that bloodline?

Exactly.

So which bloodlines could it be?

I'm not an encyclopaedia of all things Fae, we will need to do some research. My guess would be that the elders have already informed the King of this after their little experiment on you, that would explain why you have been kept so unusually close to the court.

Why would the King be bothered about my family tree though?

You're asking me why a King would be worried about a highly powerful Fae coming into his court with no allegiance to him?

She gave me a look that indicated I was being incredibly dumb.

Okay, I get that, but what is he waiting for? Why hasn't he had me killed? And why did the Prince tell me not to tell anyone if they want me dead for it?

I wish I had answers Ruby, but I don't. We need to find out where you come from, otherwise we stand no chance against them. For now, you need to dull down your efforts and make sure you don't show any more magic. The last thing we need is the King finding out you have magic, let alone strong elemental magic. We will just have to hope that the Prince is keeping it to himself, for whatever reason.

Unsurprisingly, my attempts to Internet search my heritage were unsuccessful, so I begrudgingly agreed to accompany Saffie to the castle library to research in the old-fashioned way. I was surprised to see the sheer size of the library, aisles, and aisles of books ahead of me.

First time in a library or something?

Saff, how the hell are we going to find what we need in this many books?

Maybe try asking Curtis.

She inclined her head over to the right.

Curtis?

I followed her gaze. As if sensing us looking at him, the Fae turned to stare back. He looked elderly, with beady eyes behind a pair of large circular glasses.

'Can I help you?'

As he got closer I noticed his gaze go over my ears, and suddenly his polite attitude dampened a little. Clearly another one to dislike my human appearance.

'Yes please, I'm looking to find some books on the powerful Fae families and bloodlines.'

I felt Saffie sigh next to me, and the creepy old Curtis squinted his beady eyes at me.

'And why would you be looking for books on that?'

I resisted the urge to tell him that it was none of his damn business. Instead, I forced a sickly sweet smile onto my face and replied innocently.

'I have been told that it's important to understand Fae history and more about the powerful family that I am training to protect.'

He continued to eye me, clearly mistrusting.

'Well, Aoife told me that this was where I should be looking for assistance, but if this isn't the right place then I will of course go back and inform her that you couldn't help me here.'

I continued to smile at him, and as I had hoped the mention of Aoife altered his attitude. He nodded, all be it reluctantly, and led us towards the rear of the library. Saffie gave me her impressed look this time.

Sometimes I can be strategic.

To begin with, I had been flicking aimlessly through pages, and huffing a lot at the prospect of searching endlessly through dusty old books, but as I got more into it I realised how fascinating Fae history actually was. According to the books, King Oberon's father, also named Oberon, had killed and taken over the throne from a Fae queen called Titania. Supposedly Titania's remains were locked away in a secret tomb never revealed by the original King Oberon. Something about her image drew me in.

Saff, do you know anything about Queen Titania?

No, why?

I don't know... there's something about her picture that seems familiar to me.

I turned the book to show Saffie, her blank look confirmed that she had no knowledge on the strange Queen. I turned the book back so that I could see it, and as I stared at the picture I felt a shiver run down my spine and my hair stand up on the back of my neck as though someone was breathing down it. Instinctively I shut the book. Instead, I took a minute to watch Saffie lick her paw and use it to turn pages. Fascinating.

Here we are, Titania...

Saffie nodded at a book open in front of her. I took the book and was instantly grateful that there were no pictures.

According to the book, Queen Titania was pretty savage with abducting and enslaving humans, waging wars across the realm and from what I could tell just general craziness. It says that Oberon formed an army against her and battled to take over the realm from her. But...

I paused as my eyes hovered over the next sentence.

What is it?

Saffie asked as she moved to my side to read for herself.

Oh hell. Her lineage was the only one to have access to fire magic. You're from Titania's bloodline... The revelation hung in the air between us for a moment as we took it in. From everything I had read, this was the last person I wanted to be linked to.

But hang on, if she died like 300 years ago, and everyone was killed that linked to her, how the hell did I get produced from it now?

I have no idea Saffie sounded incredibly nervous. *Come on though, we better get back, it will be dinner soon and we need time to compose ourselves before we dine with the enemy.*

Saff, it's sounding more like I am the enemy here.

Don't be ridiculous, Queen Titania may have been a monster, but don't think for one second that Oberon and his family are heroes just because they were the lesser evil.

I was getting ready for dinner when a knock at my bedroom door made me jump. I shouted for them to come in, half hoping that it was the Prince coming to fill in the details he had promised me, but instead, I was faced with Aoife.

'We need to talk.'

Her voice sounded stern for a second until she closed the door, and then her face relaxed and became inquisitive.

'What the hell happened back there?'

My breath halted as I considered for a minute that the Prince may not have kept his promise. I felt Saffie eyeing me and Aoife, her pose changing to one ready to leap into action if needed. I gulped and tried to respond calmly.

'What do you mean?'

Her perfect eyebrow raised at me, daring me to continue playing dumb, but I wasn't willing to give away anything. My life depended on it.

'The Prince and you... embracing.'

Her words came out as though she didn't quite believe it. I took a minute to internally sigh in a massive amount of relief, before taking in what she had said. I felt Saffie shift her stance once more, this time turning to plainly stare at me.

What?! You left that part out!

'I take it your pet didn't know that.'

Aoife laughed, earning a light growl from Saffie.

'I didn't think there was anything to tell, I had actually forgotten about it. I was so shaken up from the whole event and had a bit of a breakdown and he just comforted me.'

I purposefully didn't elaborate on the 'whole event' hoping she would just assume the vampire attack was it. They both continued to stare at me, clearly expecting more from me. Why was this such a big thing? No, the Prince had never come across as a hugger before, but surely comforting someone upset wasn't this much of a shocker.

'Unseelie don't do that Ruby, we aren't like you humans. I've known the Prince my entire life and have never known him to comfort anyone in general, let alone like that.'

'Well, maybe he just was giving me a break and some human-style comfort as I was on the edge of a complete meltdown.'

'No.'

She replied simply and continued staring. Saffie was still eerily quiet.

'Why does it matter? You're both making this seem so much weirder than it was.'

Whilst I appreciated that Aoife didn't know the craziest thing that had happened in that scenario, I couldn't understand her fixation on this small insignificant detail.

'Humans are so simple sometimes.'

Aoife directed this comment at Saffie, and to my shock, Saffie actually nodded in agreement. Traitor.

'Ruby, I would very surprisingly consider you a friend already, and for me to like a human is rare, but to call one a friend is unheard of. I still wouldn't consider hugging you if you began crying in front of me, it just doesn't come naturally to us.'

'So you don't hug anyone? Not even Bran?'

'He is my husband so of course I would him, but not anyone other than him and maybe some very close family members. It's just not the done thing. The Prince in particular doesn't embrace people, not even his family members.'

I couldn't find an appropriate response, and instead, I awkwardly smiled as a reflex.

'Is there something going on between you two?'

'No!'

I immediately responded, but she looked disbelieving.

'If there is, you need to stop and be very careful Ruby, the Unseelie Prince, and a half breed like you would not be well received by the King. Or any of them.'

She must have noticed the slight offense taken.

'I'm not saying it from my opinion Ruby, I just.... I care about you and I really wouldn't want to see you get hurt as a result of a bad decision. The Prince would have a tarnished reputation, but he would get over that, you wouldn't survive the scandal... The King would make sure of that.'

'Aoife, nothing is going on, I can't stress that enough.'

'Okay.'

She sighed, still clearly not buying it.

'But I want you to know that you can trust me. I am bound by my loyalty to the throne, which will always dictate my choices, but I am also loyal to my friends.'

'I would hug you for that, but I wouldn't want to freak you out.'

I smirked, and then we both laughed. She suggested that we head down to dinner.

Saffie had remained silent the whole way down, so I decided to break the tension with her.

You can't be annoyed that I didn't tell you something I didn't think mattered, especially with the gravity of the actual issues we are facing.

I'm not annoyed.

Disappointed? Raging? What is it?

I'm worried.

Well, this Titania thing is a worry I agree but...

No, not that. Aoife is right, something is going on with you and the Prince. Even if you don't realise it yet, there have been little clues and I am frustrated with myself for not noticing them sooner. This is really bad if it progresses into anything more Ruby.

Saff, this is not progressing into anything! What clues are you even on about?

We got cut off before I could get answers, as we entered the dining hall and I found my gaze making contact with the Prince's. His expression remained stern and cold, but his stare had a warmer feeling to it, sending cool tingles across my skin. Oh hell, were Saffie and Aoife right?

ASH

I had been trying not to stare at the door, waiting for her to come through it, my curiosity at an all-time high. Bran had been attempting to discuss plans for tomorrow morning's training, but I had found myself rudely drifting out of the conversation, his voice a mere bleating background noise to me. My body stiffened as soon as she entered the dining hall, led by Aoife and flanked by Saffie. A faint but invigorating odour of cinnamon and vanilla spiced up the air in the room. I hadn't noticed it from her before. The intensified expression of her powers had altered her scent to one befitting of a Fae with fire magic. I glanced around the room to see if anyone else had recognised this awakening in her. It appeared that no one had. Even Aoife, who usually was the most observant, seemed blissfully unaware as she gracefully seated herself.

Her eyes connected with mine for a brief moment and I instantly felt a warming sensation drift over the surface of my skin. The shock on her face from releasing some fire magic had been all the proof I needed to confirm to me that she was not aware of anything going on inside her. Aoife had been giving me strange looks since we had returned from the mission earlier. Bran had avoided too much eye contact and kept as strictly to business as possible. Bran had gone quiet beside me, and I glanced at Aoife who was staring at me with a gentle frown.

Dinner had proven rather uneventful, though I had felt Saffie monitoring me from over beside Ruby. I was glad to finish and get away by the end of it, but was less pleased to feel Aoife hot on my heels and following me back towards my chamber.

'Yes Aoife, can I help you with something?'

I sighed as she followed in behind me. She shut the door behind her before finally responding

'Ash.'

I turned to look at her, it was unusual for her to use my name.

'You have been my friend for as long as I can remember, you need to listen to me when I say you can't do this.'

'What exactly am I doing Aoife?'

'Ruby is not an option, she is a half-breed and it will ruin you both. Scratch that, it will damage your reputation and it will mean her death.'

My mouth went dry. I inwardly took a breath before composing myself and responding.

'Careful there Aoife, it almost sounds like you care for the human girl.'

I painted my classic arsehole smirk on, but Aoife remained unfazed. She was all too well accustomed to my behaviours.

'I do actually. Don't ask why, because I have no idea, but I want to make sure that she remains safe and that means from you as well.'

Before I could respond a knock at the door interrupted. I asked them to enter, and Bran appeared. He gave Aoife a knowing smile and closed the door behind him before taking a stance next to his wife.

'Ash...'

'Oh, not you too.'

I groaned as my best friend gave me a look indicating he was about to back up his wife's argument.

'If anyone other than Aoife and I had been there today, what rumours do you think would be flying around? As it is, I don't care either way about Ruby Goodall and how she fares here, but I do care about you and it is my job to protect you, particularly as your best friend and second in command.'

'Do you really think I am weak to such emotions?'

I began to feel defensive, and as such I took back my commanding tone and decided to remind them of their position.

'I am the Unseelie Prince and I do not need regulating or reigning in by either of you. I do not need to explain my decisions, but rest assured my interests in the human are not what you are thinking.'

They both glanced at each other briefly before nodding at me and bowing their heads.

'You can both leave now.'

With that, they obediently exited and left me alone. I was not keen on using my status over my friends, but I was not about to stand for being reprimanded by them.

I mulled over my conflicting emotions for a while after they left. My title meant that the decision should be simple. I should go to the King and inform him of this new development with Ruby. She was, after all, a prisoner. That was also the role entrusted to me as a weapon of the crown. However, my gut instinct was telling me that she was innocent in this all and that she didn't deserve the fate awaiting her. Life had been much simpler before meeting her. My role had been simple, and my future was guaranteed. Now though, I was left contemplating betraying my King and likely risking my own life. My father would see me dead before he allowed any risk to come to his position of power.

CHAPTER NINE

RUBY

A couple of days had passed with minimal contact with the Prince, even Aoife had seemed slightly distant. Thankfully Oakley had been there to offer himself up as a sparring partner for training and a friend to talk to so that I didn't go insane from loneliness when Saffie wasn't around. Saffie had been out a lot more recently, in search of answers for our ever-accumulating questions about my heritage and the infamous Queen Titania. I sat patiently in my bedroom after training, waiting for Saffie to return, when the beeping of my phone made me jump and pulled me out of my thoughts.

"Hi Rubes! I just wanted to check that you're still coming tonight as none of us had heard much from you in a couple of weeks? Xxx" The text from Faye made my stomach turn, how was I supposed to tell her that I was unlikely to be allowed out to her engagement party because I was being held hostage by faeries? She wouldn't forgive me if I didn't make it. A knock at the door pulled my attention from my phone, and I shouted to come in.

'Hello.'

The Prince's voice sounded velvety smooth as he swung the door open and leaned against the frame. I really wished his voice wasn't making me tingle, and my throat dry up. I managed a semi-smile and nod. That natural cocky smirk appeared in response to my very obvious reaction to him. 'It's probably time we talked.'

He finally crossed the threshold, closing the door behind him. I squirmed awkwardly as he made his way over to me and perched at the end of my bed.

'I know I'm a descendent of the Queen Titania.'

His eyebrow raised in a brief look of surprise.

'Someone has done some research by the seems of it.'

'It turns out only one person's bloodline could do what I did the other day. Or so the books suggested anyway?'

I probed, half hoping that he would say that the books were wrong.

'The books are correct to my knowledge.'

'Then why am I still alive? Your type don't seem to be the most risk-taking with potential threats.' My voice trembled ever so slightly as I began to question if he was here for exactly that reason.

'Don't panic Ruby, if I wanted to kill you then you would have been dead already.'

He lightly chuckled, but unsurprisingly it didn't make me feel better.

'I have no intention of letting anyone find out, that's why I needed to speak with you and explain why it's crucial that you get better control of your powers. If anyone else finds out, I won't be able to protect you. You will be killed.'

'I don't understand any of it. Titania was killed

hundreds of years ago, her bloodline was wiped out according to the books. How can I possibly have anything to do with her?'

'That is something I don't yet know the answers to either, but I am trying to find out... whilst being discreet.'

'And why would you be looking to protect me?'

Whilst I'd like to have believed that there were some good intentions here, I had to be sensible and expect an ulterior motive. The Unseelie, from what I had seen, weren't the most generous and loving creatures. He paused and watched me for a few seconds before answering.

'Call it curiosity if you like.'

He answered flippantly and glanced away.

'So what do I do now? How do I get control of this?'

'We need to know what you're capable of, test your powers, and find out how much we need to work on controlling.'

'And how do I know you're not finding this out for your father, and planning to kill me after?'

'You don't. I guess you will just have to trust me and find out.'

He shrugged, nonchalant. It didn't help to reassure me.

'Well, that's reassuring. How are we going to do that without others finding out about me then?'

'We will have to do some training in secret, out of the watch of anyone else.'

Whilst he was explaining to me his ideas of where would be best to conduct this secret training, I received another text, which a glance at the phone told me was from Marie. Damn it, I might as well ask him now, there wasn't going to be a better time.

'One of my best friends is engaged.'

'Okay?'

He looked confused. My nerves were making it significantly harder to be coherent in my approach to the topic.

'There's an engagement party for her and I am supposed to be attending, as I'm a bridesmaid.'

He continued to watch me, waiting for an elaboration.

'I am asking to be released for just a few hours so that I can celebrate with my friend and pretend for one evening that I am normal again?'

'You want to go play human whilst all of this is going on?'

He gave me a look that suggested he thought I was stupid.

'I get that it doesn't mean anything to someone like you, but this is my life, and one that I may not have much left of depending on how things progress. I just want to celebrate with my friends and be able to forget for one evening that my life has gone to hell. I was planning to ask Oakley to come with me and chaperone if that helps at all?'

I felt a little bad for volunteering Oakley up to babysit me, but needs must. The Prince gave me a strange look.

'Why would you choose Oakley to accompany you?'

There was no hint of malice in his question, just genuine intrigue.

'He's my friend. Plus it looks normal to turn up with a date, so it wouldn't be suspicious. My friends will be incredibly worried if I don't attend this. It would definitely draw attention to my lack of presence in the human world.'

'You can go.'

His answer was short, but I couldn't help the massive grin that spread instantly across my face. I was about to shower him with thank-yous, when he continued.

'But I will be coming, not Oakley.'

'Why?'

The thought of this beautiful but awkward creature accompanying me rather than my friend was a little deflating for the prospect of having fun and feeling normal.

'If anything happens I will need to be able to manage the situation, I can't leave a ticking time bomb like you under the supervision of someone incapable of dealing with you.'

I was about to jump to Oakley's and my own defence, but he swiftly got up and left before I had the chance.

Saffie had been eyeing me strangely since I had told her what the plan for the evening was. She was annoyed at first that I said she couldn't come with me, but she eventually agreed it would look super weird to take my cat with me to a party.

'Saff please stop eyeballing my every movement, what is your issue?'

I sighed whilst running some curling irons through my hair.

Getting dressed up to be accompanied out by the Prince, are we?

Sarcasm oozed from her. It was starting to get annoying.

Or I'm getting dressed up as a bridesmaid at my friend's engagement party. I told you, nothing is going on and nothing will go on.

She just nodded and continued to watch me, so I decided to stop paying attention to her judgemental presence and focus on making myself feel more like a human girl again, getting ready for a party. I had settled on a blue sequined cocktail dress, some black strappy heels, and a simple smoky-eyed look. Twirling in front of the mirror I couldn't help but smile, feeling just a bit more like my old self again, finally.

You look beautiful Ruby.

Saffie commented genuinely from behind me, breaking the hour-and-a-half silence we had shared. I turned and smiled warmly at her before making the move to give her a big hug. A knock on the door broke us out of embrace and I was confronted with the stunningly beautiful Fae prince. My eyes trailed down him and back up again, stopping suddenly on his ears.

'Your ears!?'

My voice came out as alarmed as I felt. His unusual pointed tops had disappeared and instead, the features looked human.

'It's a spell, I can't really go around the human world not looking human can I? Ready to go?'

He chuckled in response. Whilst the Prince may be under the impression his ear change would help to make him look human, he was underestimating how much his beauty added to his supernatural appearance. But, I wasn't about to inflate his ego further by expressing that, so I smiled sweetly and nodded instead.

We took a portal to my house, so that nothing out of the ordinary would be witnessed, with the intention of getting a taxi to the party. The prince stood awkwardly in the hallway until I told him to just go and sit in the living room, and after throwing out the very out-of-date fridge items I joined him whilst we waited for our taxi. The ride was only ten minutes as I lived quite close to Faye. As we got out of the taxi I was surprised to see the Prince almost appeared nervous.

'Are you worried or something?'''

I asked playfully, and he squinted his eyes at me in an unimpressed fashion.

'It's not exactly within my comfort zone; mingling with an entire room of humans.'

'Just try not to insult anyone or say anything too weird. In fact, probably try to avoid talking too much.'

I laughed, enjoying his discomfort a little too much. After all the mocking I had received since being at the Unseelie court, for being 'that human girl' who knew nothing, I could finally be in control and watch one of them squirm a bit. He bit back a retort and instead followed me inside, remaining quiet.

Inside I was greeted immediately with a huge hug from Faye who already looked like she might have had a few glasses of wine.

'I'm so glad you made it!'

Her voice reached squealing level, before her eyes drifted over to the prince who was standing uncomfortably next to me.

'And who is this?'

Her mouth dropped open slightly as she took in his radiant beauty. I couldn't blame her, I still wasn't used to it.

'This is...'

I began, before realising I couldn't address him as the Prince. Damn. I hesitated and glanced at him, trying to think up an introduction on the spot.

'I'm Ash.'

He suddenly spoke up, and to my surprise extended his hand with a confident and charming grin. I had to force my own mouth closed. Faye hesitated for a moment, and then pulled herself together enough to smile back and accept the handshake. Faye's fiancé came over then, gave me a brief hug and shook hands with the Prince. He managed to swoop the Prince off towards the kitchen with promises of them returning to us with drinks. The second they left, Faye spun on the spot and widened her eyes at me.

'Oh my god Rubes! He is absolutely gorgeous!'

Her voice took on that exceptionally high-pitched tone again. I couldn't help but laugh, I had so missed this sort of friend.

'Where the hell did you find him?'

Whilst it would have been lovely to be able to tell her everything, and get everything off my chest, there was no way that that was an option. I hated to admit that the Prince was right, but on this he was. Humans could not handle the truth. I barely could, and apparently I was only half human. So, I settled with a plausibly boring story.

'He came in to the restaurant one evening, and asked for my number, and it just went from there.'

The other girls arrived just in time to hear, and they joined in with Faye's squeals of excitement at the stunning stranger I had brought to the party. Ash, he had said his name was Ash. Was that made up, or potentially his real name? My eyes wandered across the room to find him as I zoned out unintentionally from the conversation that had moved on to Faye's wedding dress. He looked so natural as he leaned against the breakfast bar, sipping a beer and laughing with a group of guys. As if he could feel my gaze, his eyes turned and met with mine, and that all too familiar shiver ran down my spine and across my skin.

I felt my cheeks blush as he made his way back towards us, acutely aware that the girls had noticed the intense stare I had held with him. He stood by my side, arm brushing against mine. After that we conversed for a couple of hours with the other guests and indulged in plenty of drinks, not talking much to each other but keeping close enough to be nearly touching. The longer the night went on, and the more drinks we consumed, the more we exchanged flirtatious looks. The sensible part of my brain was telling me to be careful and remember Aoife's warning, but the rest of me was enjoying the interactions far too much with the world's most sexy creature ever created.

ASH

As the evening went on I felt myself relax into the environment and even found myself sharing one or two genuine laughs with Ruby's human friends. It became obvious that Ruby was capable of lighting up any room she entered and making any circumstance enjoyable. I had never seen her so happy and genuinely herself, and I couldn't help but feel a slight sense of guilt and sadness. She had been happy. I hadn't understood it before, but I felt like this insight into her previous life was a rather rude awakening for me. I could only be further impressed with her resilience and ability to embrace and adapt to everything. Whilst I silently reflected and lost myself in thought, I clearly lost track of Ruby. As I regained my attention on the room my heart raced a little as I realised that she was not where I thought she was. I turned quickly, my Fae senses regained as I felt ready to tear apart the whole room searching for her. Immediately I breathed a sigh of relief as I bumped straight into her. Then I noticed her hand extended. Her cheeks were flushed from the alcohol.

'We are dancing.'

'No.'

I responded instantly. Her lips contorted to a pout.

'Yes. You want to look human right? Everyone else is dancing.'

Her voice had lowered but there was a strong hint of challenge in her tone. Her hand gestured towards the crowd of people drinking and dancing merrily. The girl certainly had the Fae manipulation skill ingrained in her.

'Fine.'

I smirked and ensured my voice sounded confident when accepting her challenge. Internally however I was concerned. Her friends performed an excessive squeal of excitement as Ruby led me toward them. I smiled through my discomfort. They waved their arms and sang out of tune to whatever song was playing. Their drinks sloshed over the sides of their glasses. Their fingers stroked my arm and grabbed at me, and the urge to recoil was tough to keep in check. Perhaps I should have allowed Oakley to take this role after all. I couldn't put my finger on it, but something was off with Oakley since Ruby had arrived. He had been interested in her from the moment she had arrived, ensuring that he was present when possible with her. Whilst Ruby did appear to have an interesting effect on many, there was something I didn't like about the change in Oakley. Fingers stroked down my hand, cutting off my train of thought. I instantly knew Ruby's touch though and warmed as she pulled me closer to her. The new song had a slower pace, and I noticed that everyone split away into couples to dance. Ruby slung her arms around my neck and I followed suit by placing my hands on her waist. Our eyes met briefly, but I tore my gaze away quickly. Instead, we danced with each other silently and looked past one another. An unspoken understanding of the situation's inappropriate-ness hung thick in the air.

CHAPTER TEN

RUBY

The taxi ride back to my house was practically silent at first, until my discomfort manifested into uncontrollable talking. My mind was begging me to stop but my mouth just carried on as I chattered on about my friends, Faye's house, the food, and the gossip I had heard. Meanwhile, the Prince just sat uncomfortably staring out of the window. The journey, whilst short, felt like a lifetime.

He finally broke his long silence as we entered through the front door of my home.

'Are you ready to go back?'

He sounded distant, though not unfriendly.

'Yes, I just need to grab some bits from upstairs first.'

I went to turn away but his fingers wrapped gently around my wrist and pulled me back to face him. Our faces nearly touching, I could feel his breath on my lips, and I licked mine in response. I tilted my head slightly towards him in expectation. He hesitated for a moment, conflict raging in his eyes in the most transparent moment I had encountered with him before. Then it was gone. That stony stare and unfazed but clinical expression resumed. Had I completely misread the situation?

'What are you doing?'

My words were barely audible.

'I will wait in here.'

His words were rigid as he dropped contact with me and strolled off into the living room. A feverish embarrassment spread rapidly across my entire face. What kind of fool was I to react like that to him? To avoid any further issues I ran up the stairs two at a time to my bedroom.

The embarrassment of rejection was stinging a bit too much, and so I tried to take a deep breath and focus my brain on what I had wanted to retrieve from my bedroom.

'Come on Ruby, get it together.'

I scolded myself out loud. My eyes scoured over my old bedroom, remembering how much simpler life had been before. A tear started to form in my eye at the realisation that I would never be able to return to this level of comfort and normality. My observation came to a screeching halt when I noticed the open drawers, and items sprawled out over the dressing table. An unnerving feeling spread through me. I stepped closer to inspect and saw that my drawer of photos had been emptied and gone through.

'Help!'

I shouted at the top of my voice, unsure what else to do. The Prince immediately came sprinting up and appeared at my side, eyes frantically searching for a threat. I pointed at the photo collection, and he gave me once again a confused look after realising I was not being attacked.

'Please tell me this was your lot that did this when they collected my things for me before.'

I knew the answer but his instantly furrowed brow and

head shake confirmed my worries. Someone had been in my house. It would have been terrifying enough if I had thought it was an ordinary burglary, but my gut was telling me that this was supernatural.

'I was here for that, this wasn't them.'

'Then who the hell has been in my house, rooting through my bedroom drawers like some sort of stalker? They've taken my photos out!'

My voice was starting to get a bit shrill and fast-paced as the worrying realisations and questions flooded my mind.

'Ruby I'm going to need you to check everything and see if anything has actually been taken.'

The prince ordered as he frowned looking around the room.

Despite my mind being in overdrive, and my hands shaking, I managed to sift through the photos and was able to confirm that a few were missing. I made my way around the room and informed the Prince that my heart necklace from my dead mother, and my hair brush had been taken.

'Photos and personal items, that could be a witchcraft thing.'

He grumbled, seeming increasingly concerned. His fingers sifted through his hair and I could practically see his mind working at maximum capacity.

'What would witches want with me?'

'One witch, well as far as we are aware.'

He corrected.

'Katherine Sparrow'

'What would this Katherine Sparrow want with me?'

My voice was noticeably shaking now.

'We don't know why, but we believe she is working in conjunction with Viktor.'

The words made my blood run cold.

'What does that sicko want with me? Why won't he leave me alone?'

I whispered. Noting my fear he wrapped his arms around me.

'I will not let him near you again Ruby. I will find him, and I will kill him.'

His voice was solid and protective. I buried my face into his chest, relishing the comfort of his embrace once again.

The portal back to the castle did not help the excessively nauseating sensation that had built from the stress of the situation. As soon as we arrived I began to walk towards my room, but the Prince stopped me and inclined his head to suggest I follow him. I glanced briefly in the direction of my room, wishing I could go there and just bury my head into the pillow, but instead I obediently followed. He led me to his room, which was impressive, to say the least. I didn't think it would be possible to make my room here at the castle look cheap, but the Prince's room managed it. He gestured for me to take a seat on the sofa, and so I did. He exchanged a brief few words quietly on the phone, and five minutes later Aoife, Bran, and Saffie all turned up to the room. Aoife and Bran had calm expressions, but Saffie was the giveaway as she oozed worry through our connection.

Ruby, what's going on?

Before I could answer, the Prince cleared his throat and eyed us pointedly, clearly expecting us to make our conversations open to the group.

'I wanted to call a meeting between the five of us as some new concerns have come to light. It appears Viktor's interest in Ruby has become more pronounced, as he has stolen some personal items of hers from her human home.'

All eyes turned to look at me.

'What would be the interest in this human?'

Bran questioned, looking almost surprised that I could be worth anything to anyone. I took a mild offense to his insinuation but managed to hold my tongue. The Prince gave me an uncomfortable look, and I could instantly tell he was considering whether to tell them about my new found powers. I nodded to him lightly, giving my consent, for what it was worth, to tell them.

'There is more to Ruby, we have discovered, than was previously realised. I need to know that you both will take this information no further than the confines of this group.'

His voice had taken on the stern and authoritative tone that I doubted anyone would risk going against.

'We are loyal to you, Prince.'

Bran answered with complete loyalty and devotion in his voice, Aoife's expression mirrored her husband's words. It was incredible really to witness the amazing connection these Fae soldiers had with their leader. The Prince hesitated for a moment before sighing and speaking again

'Ruby is from Queen Titania's bloodline, and she appears to have inherited her affinity and ability to use fire magic.'

Bran and Aoife's faces lost their composure and they looked completely lost for words. Aoife's eyes darted questioningly towards me, a slight hint of disappointment evident that I could only assume was because I hadn't entrusted her with the information myself. Saffie was plastered to my side, her eyes narrowed and assessing each Fae in the room, ready to take on anyone that posed a threat. Bran eventually broke the silence first.

'What is your plan?'

His question was directed at the Prince and he was keeping his focus completely on his commander. Aoife, however, carried on looking between me and the Prince.

'I need all of your help In protecting her and ensuring that no one else finds out.'

He then took a breath before staring each of the Fae directly in the eyes.

'Especially the King.'

They both shuffled uncomfortably, clearly unsure about hiding something from the King.

'You follow my orders, remember that.'

His voice remained commanding, and they both nodded in return.

'We also need to find Viktor and Katherine, and stop whatever they're planning.'

TWO WEEKS LATER

Since the group meeting the Prince, Bran, and Aoife had all acted more strangely towards me. I had been kept close to them at all times. For all missions I had been in their group, and for training I remained paired with Aoife to ensure I didn't accidentally overdo my efforts. The Prince had not mentioned our unusual interaction again either, but I could feel him watching me, and my body reacted longingly despite me wishing it wouldn't. Despite my feelings of utter embarrassment around the Prince, I was determined to develop with my magic. The Prince had been working secretly with me, trying to coax it out of me so that he could help me harness and control it better. Unfortunately, there were no signs that there had ever even been magic within me.

I was on my way back to my room after an evening training session when Oakley caught up to me. I hadn't spent much time with him since being under close surveillance.

'Hey Ruby, do you want to do something tonight?'

He grinned at me. I briefly considered how much trouble I would be in, but brushed it off quickly. He was part of the King's guard, so I would be safe enough.

'Sure, how about the gardens? We could go for an evening walk?'

'Excellent, I will sneak some of the wine from the kitchen and head out to the deeper parts of the garden for a secret drink.'

He winked and then grinned again. It seemed uncharacteristic for Oakley but I was nothing short of grateful for it after the recent events.

I had already used my connection to let Saffie know where I was going, to prevent her worrying and tearing the castle apart looking for me. However, I did ignore her excessive nagging and worrying responses. He led me through the gardens, the sprites ignoring us as we avoided getting in their busy way. Oakley indicated going off track and held some branches out of the way for me to scramble through the thick bush area. As I emerged I couldn't help but gasp as I was presented with a beautiful area of grass interspersed with gorgeous bright blue flowers, a pond, and small fountain to the left.

'This is beautiful.'

I commented as Oakley emerged through the bush next to me.

'I love it here, it's so peaceful.'

I followed him to a space next to the fountain and sat beside him. We both reclined back onto our forearms and shared taking swigs from the bottle of wine.

'So how are you finding it here now? Still feeling like a helpless hostage?'

'I still feel like a hostage as I have no freedom, but I am starting to get used to it here, to be honest. I like training, and feeling strong.'

'You're getting much better now, Aoife isn't able to kick your arse as hard as she used to.'

He chuckled, and I poked my tongue out before jokingly pushing him.

'Careful you nearly spilled the wine.'

He laughed even harder and nearly choked on his mouthful.

'I haven't seen you much lately though, seriously is everything okay? I feel like I've missed something.'

His laughter turned more serious and concerned. I desperately wanted to tell him the truth, but the Prince had been very clear that I wasn't to let anyone else know, and my life depended on it.

'Everything is fine.'

I smiled hoping it would reassure him, but it didn't seem to.

'I guess I'm being monitored more closely as I am meant to be showing them something I haven't yet, as I'm still very clearly human and not progressing like someone with Fae abilities.'

The lie felt wrong. He nodded though and seemed to accept my explanation. We spent a couple of hours laughing and drinking, just enjoying and relaxing in one another's company before finally making our way back. There was something so refreshing about our friendship, he made me almost feel normal again and I couldn't help but smile and be grateful for having met him.

As I entered my room, I wasn't expecting to see anyone

as Saffie had already told me she was going out to hunt in the forests surrounding the castle for a while. So I had to stifle a scream when I entered, humming to myself, and came face to face with a very distressed-looking Fae.

'Where have you been?'

The Prince fumed.

'I was with a friend, having a drink.'

I stammered, still in shock. His eyes widened in response.

'I was only in the gardens!'

Thankfully his bulging eyes reverted.

'You had me very worried Ruby.'

The intensity of his stare was starting to stir a reaction in me again. Damn body.

'I was only with Oakley, we were just having a relaxed evening after training.'

A flash of what would have, if he were any other guy, looked like jealousy crossed his face.

'Oakley?"

'Yes, Oakley, he's my friend.'

'I see.'

His eyes dipped to the floor momentarily.

'I apologise for entering uninvited, but please be sure not to venture off with anyone other than myself, Aoife, or Bran anymore. It is not safe. There is still so much unknown and we should not be taking any unnecessary risks.'

With that, he left the room, and I was left standing completely baffled. The male gender had been a mystery to me in the human world, but Fae men were considerably worse.

CHAPTER ELEVEN

ASH

Private training with Ruby today had been an awkward experience. I had needed to actively remind myself to avert my attention from Ruby. There was something unique and fascinating about her that just drew my attention completely. I had contemplated cancelling the session, but considering the magnitude of the situation I could not justify avoiding working on her magic with her. I took the opportunity, whilst walking down the halls afterward, to try to mentally shake myself. What was it about her that made me feel so out of control? I had never been one for lacking self-control until now. I had never questioned myself or my orders before. As I entered my room I was surprised to see my father.

'Where have you been?!'

His face was reddening with frustration, and he paused what appeared to have been pacing. Before I could answer though he continued

'We have had information that Viktor Adley is in the forests outside the castle, with reinforcements.'

This was alarming.

'How far out are they?'

'We are unsure. But they don't appear to be moving in, we aren't clear on their intentions. They must be apprehended immediately.'

The king ordered. I nodded and agreed to gather the king's guard. As soon as my father left, I called Bran for assistance in composing a strategy and assembling the appropriate teams. He was up in my room within a couple of minutes.

'Prince, we need to leave Ruby here, it wouldn't be wise to take her into that situation. Aside from the obvious dangers, there is also the risk that under that pressure she may expel some magic that you wouldn't want others to see.'

Bran wasn't wrong, but the thought of leaving her unsupervised made me feel sick. I took a moment to weigh up my options.

'Okay, I want Aoife here with her in the group that will be protecting the castle grounds. Go gather everyone on our team and get ready we leave in 20 minutes."

He swiftly left on my command and I gave it a couple of minutes before I headed out and towards Ruby's room to warn her.

'So Viktor is near us?'

Ruby's voice had escalated in pitch, and her eyes were nervously surveying the room as if Viktor could jump out of anywhere.

'You will be staying in the group here, and I've ordered Aoife to be here with you just In case.'

She nodded nervously, still clearly mentally pacing.

'Ruby, we will apprehend him.'

I touched her cheek gently and pulled her face to look at me. Those beautiful eyes gazed into mine as she breathed a sigh and half smiled at me trustingly.

How do you know this isn't a trap? Saffie's voice growled at me and I immediately dropped my hand, recognizing my mistake.

'I don't, hence why I have ordered Aoife to stay with her.'

She glared over at me from Ruby's bed.

'Be careful.'

Ruby's words caught my attention back from the glaring feline. Her obvious concern for me made me smile inwardly. I could feel the tension between Saffie and Ruby as I left.

With Bran in my shadow and the rest of our team behind him, I led the group through the forest. There was an eerie quiet to it. Normally the woodland creatures would be going about their business and creating a crunch of the ground, or a rustle of the trees, or a calling to one another. Today, however, there was nothing. My instincts were screaming danger alarms at me, and my fingers tightened around the handle of my sword.

'To the left!'

A voice from behind shouted. I turned just in time to see a figure rushing forward, fangs flashed out at us. Bran was in front of me instantly, sword drawn and slicing forward at the figure. As if it had been a cue for others, more came rushing through the trees at us.

RUBY

My hands had been shaking since the Prince had told me that Viktor was nearby, but I was trying to hide it from the others. Saffie had transitioned into her Panther form just in case her intuition was right and it was, in fact, a setup. Sensing my nerves Aoife suggested that we go to my room and relax there for a while, to which I agreed in the hope that the comforts of my own room would ease my tension.

'Ruby, it's going to be fine, they will get him.'

Aoife was doing her best to be reassuring, but a feeling in my stomach was telling me there was something wrong.

'Saffie, for the love of all that is Fae, please stop with your incessant pacing.'

Aoife groaned at Saffie, who in response just rolled her eyes and slumped down by my side with a huff. Whilst I didn't like to agree with someone moaning at my familiar, having a panther pace a couple of steps in each direction for ten minutes straight in a confined space was not the most relaxing or comforting. I could tell she was feeling just as anxious as I was. I wished I could know what was happening. Had they found Viktor? Was the Prince okay? Saffie's head lifted and her ears pricked up.

Someone is coming

She alerted us. We all stared at the door expectantly and were surprised to see Oakley burst through. His eyes were wide, and he looked very worried.

'Aoife, the castle is under attack!'

Aoife jumped to her feet and ordered him to gather weapons. As she was about to hurry out with him, she span on the spot to look at me and commanded me to stay put in my room no matter what. I nodded sheepishly, happy to follow that order. Then she was gone.

The sounds of battle outside my window made me tremble even further, and I scurried to the window to take a peek.

Ruby get away from the windows.

Saffie hissed at me.

Oh my god, there are more Fae out there.

Yes Ruby, they will be the ones fighting to defend the castle.

No smart arse, as in they are fighting other Fae that are attacking the castle.

Saffie's eyes grew wide and she quickly strode over to take a look also. It wasn't hard to tell the castle's defence from the attackers, the intruder Fae were not dressed in the same armour and castle colours as our lot. I searched the crowd for Aoife and Oakley but couldn't see them anywhere. A crashing of someone coming flying through my door made me and Saffie spin around instantly. Saffie immediately positioned herself in front of me, ready to attack. Wood had splintered off in all directions, and I gasped to see Aoife drag her injured body up from the floor.

'Little help here Saffie!'

She shouted as a huge creature appeared in the hallway. The dark, swampy green giant roared furiously. Its head was hunched slightly as it struggled to fully fit within the confines of the building. I recoiled in sheer horror at the grotesque thing. An overwhelmingly strong odour of rotting moss and vegetation filled the air around us, and I choked back a sudden urge to retch.

Oh god, it's a troll!

Was all Saffie said before she launched, claws and teeth out at the creature. She must have connected with it as it released an ear-piercing shriek before it attempted to batter her with its oversized club-like hands. I found myself pinned to the wall, watching and unable to move. Aoife bobbed and weaved between its continuous swings, whilst Saffie clung onto its back like a leech, her teeth chomping away into him. They had moved with the creature back out into the hallway, but with the oversized hole in the door and wall, I could still see what was happening. I begged for my magic to spark up so that I could help my friends, but it didn't respond. A gentle humming noise distracted me from the scene ahead, and then out of nowhere a portal formed in the doorway, and out came a middle-aged woman with bright red hair and piercing green feline eyes.

'You must be Ruby.'

She sneered, an air of evil about her.

'Ruby, Run!'

I heard Aoife's voice scream through at me before she took another hit that sent her flying down the hall and out of my sight. I made a move to try to dart around the woman in front of me, but with a flick of her hand, she had me thrown backwards and pinned to the wall. My neck twanged painfully as it connected with the wall, and I gritted my teeth in response.

'Katherine I presume?'

I groaned, trying to breathe through the slightly winded feeling.

'Indeed I am!'

She cackled at me.

'And you're the not-so-human girl we have been trying to get hold of. Slippery little one aren't you, hiding here and making life far more difficult than it needed to be.'

I resisted the urge to correct her choice of words, as hiding was not what I would call my situation.

'What does Viktor want with me?'

I demanded, anger just about overriding my fear. One

of her brows arched into a confused look.

'Viktor? My dear, Viktor would have just drained you and moved on if we were going along with his plan. He is merely a pawn in our master's plan for you.'

Suddenly the fear was back. If there was a plan for me, and Viktor was not the head bad guy, then this really wasn't good.

'Now that's enough chit-chat, time to come with me.'

Her hand extended out in front of her and she created a portal.

'Not a chance!'

I shouted, panicking and writhing against her invisible hold on me. There was absolutely no way that I was going to go willingly to what I could only assume was to be significantly worse than here. It took a minute, but with some serious thrashing her hold broke and I dropped to the floor in time to try to make a break for the door. Her hand grabbed at my hair though and dragged me backwards. My back crashed against the floor with a thud and she was instantly over me, hand gripped around my throat.

'You can either come nicely or I will happily drag your body unconscious and beaten.'

She spat at me. My scalp felt alight with pain, and I was struggling to breathe. I suddenly felt the familiar warming sensation run through me as my body seemed to inwardly charge itself, realising the threat finally and reacting. From the corner of my eye, I saw Oakley appear behind her, his face startled. The glow spread out of me and exploded, throwing Katherine off me and slashing at her as though I had thrown glass shards at her. Screams erupted from her, and her shock was enough to allow me to get onto my feet again. I raised my hands, ready to attack again, but before I could she withdrew a knife from her waistband, grabbed Oakley, and held it to his throat.

'No!'

Before I could do anything she slipped through the portal with him, and they were gone. I dropped to my knees, breathless and in a state of shock.

Just seconds later Aoife and Saffie burst into the open hole that had previously been my door, Saffie releasing a huge roar. The ogre's lifeless body lay bloodied in the hallway. Aoife was covered in cuts and pieces of the castle walls. Saffie's stance was uncomfortable, holding one of her paws slightly off the ground, pain obvious.

Ruby, are you ok? Did she hurt you?

'She took him! She took Oakley!'

Tears burst through.

'I couldn't stop her.'

Saffie hurried to my side and nuzzled at my arm. I flung my arms around her neck and sobbed uncontrollably. Aoife gave me all of about 2 minutes before she dragged me away and forced me to look at her.

'I need you to tell me everything that was said.'

CHAPTER TWELVE

RUBY

It felt like forever until the Prince and Bran returned and made it back to the castle where Aoife, Saffie, and I were sat desperately waiting. Bran's eyes went wide and a look of worry flashed over his face as he took in his wife's appearance. Rips in her clothes, dried blood sticking them to her body and already rising bumps and bruises visible. He didn't say anything, but immediately moved to her side and gave her a meaningful look. It was such a beautiful and subtle relationship to witness. The Prince gave her a respectful and almost grateful nod of appreciation, which she returned. His attention turned to me and Saffie then. My poor familiar looked in a pretty beaten-up shape too, but she was refusing to acknowledge or show her discomfort too much. His eyes roamed over me, and he appeared relieved to see that I had come out of the situation pretty unscathed. They immediately launched into a quick run down of events from their end.

'We were surrounded by mostly newly turned

vampires, which were easy enough to overcome but it was just the sheer quantity of them that made it take so long. Viktor had already disappeared by the time we had arrived.'

Bran sounded very frustrated.

'What happened here?'

The Prince asked cautiously, taking another glance at the troll corpse in the hallway and the castle's internal destruction. Aoife turned to me and indicated that I needed to fill them in, so I did my best to retell the events as thoroughly but quickly as I could.

'So how do we find Oakley?'

I asked after I had finished. I felt the others avert their gaze awkwardly, the Prince looked uncomfortable and shifted on his feet before answering me.

'We won't be going to find him, Ruby. It's clearly a trap, and so to send others into the firing line for a Fae that is likely already dead by now is just completely counterproductive.'

I stared incredulously at him for a moment, before glancing at Aoife and Bran in the hope they would be just as shocked as me. They were not. Aoife gave me a mildly sympathetic look, and Bran just seemed nonchalant. Sometimes it was easy to forget the differences between myself and the Fae went deeper than our appearances, this was not one of those times.

'You're going to leave him to die?!'

My voice rose with my temper.

'What happened to looking after our own? What happened to loyalty?!'

The Prince seemed somewhat irritated but averted his line of sight.

'Ruby, we care but every guard knows what the risks are

and their loyalty is to the throne. Oakley understands his duty, as we all do.'

Aoife responded to me. I couldn't hide the feeling of disappointment towards her especially.

'You are all so wrong.'

I shook my head, absolute disbelief making me unsure what else to say. It was at that point they seemed to tune me out and discuss their assumptions about what was being planned and what would happen. I glanced towards Saffie who looked just as disgusted as me.

What is wrong with them? How can they not care?

That's Fae for you.

Saffie sounded unhappy with them, but also generally exhausted.

Saff, you need to rest, you've taken a complete battering today. Can I get you anything?

The sound of her exhaustion started to worry me. I began to really take in her heavy eyes, cuts, and grazes that had leaked enough blood to stick her black fur into heavy matts.

'As we clearly are not needed, can you lot take this to a different room? My familiar is needing to rest.'

My tone was short and abrasive but I couldn't care at that moment. I had enough on my mind with Saffie being injured, and one of my closest Fae friends abducted. Bran left without saying a word, the Prince gave me a strange look before leaving silently too, and Aoife strangely touched my arm and commented that she was glad I was okay before following the others.

I encouraged Saffie to visit Samira for treatment and healing help, which thankfully she agreed to. I laid on my bed, not wanting to go down for dinner, and I couldn't stop my head from replaying the day's events, in particular the look on Oakley's face. Guilt was eating me up. I should have reacted faster. I should have used my powers to save him. It should have been me taken and facing death, not him. Was the Prince right, was he likely already dead? Tears stung at my eyes again. A sudden bang on the window made me jump up off the bed, my heart hammering in my chest. Once my eyes focussed I realised that it was a Raven perched on the outside window ledge, knocking its beak on the glass. Its beady black eyes stared into mine, and I could tell instantly it was a familiar. My gut instinct said not to open it and to run and find the Prince, but my curiosity peaked higher and I went over to let the creature in. It hopped in and stood in the centre of my room, still staring at me.

'Who are you?'

I asked aloud.

I am Gertrude, familiar of Katherine Sparrow.

My pulse quickened ever further, a sweat starting to form on my skin. This was not good. I glanced towards the door, contemplating running for help.

I wouldn't if I were you, not if you want to save your precious Fae friend.

'What have you done to him?'

I spat, glaring at the evil bird.

Oh don't worry about that, he is alive for now, but he won't be for long.

What do you want?

I felt the desperation to save him overwhelming the other warning thoughts in my head. As soon as I had asked, a portal appeared in the corner of the room.

Take that portal, and you will have a chance to save him. His life for yours.

The bird sang in a sadistic way.

You've got to be kidding, why the hell would I go through that portal? You lot will kill me instantly!

Well, unless you want your friend to die because of you? And I would hurry, this offer is time limited and is just for you.

The bird gave me a look to show that I wasn't going to be able to get help and save Oakley. I had to make a choice. Who was I kidding, there was no choice, he didn't deserve to die because of me. Giving a final glare to Gertrude, I took a deep breath and ran through the portal.

I landed on my knees on the other side, a nauseous feeling threatening my stomach. Concrete and stones stabbed into my knees and shins. That portal had felt very different from the others I had experienced, and I wasn't a fan. Looking around I realised suddenly that I wasn't alone. Viktor's face was the one I saw first, that sickening and devilish smile showing his fangs. He looked hungrier with each second we made eye contact. Next to him stood Katherine, amusement on her lips.

'Welcome Ruby.'

Katherine's voice broke my attention away from Viktor. The portal was a mistake. Oakley was nowhere to be seen, and they had me trapped.

'Where is he?'

I demanded as I stumbled to my feet. My attempt to sound even remotely strong or threatening was likely laughable to them. Katherine grinned at this,

'Oakley darling, come in.'

I heard footsteps behind me and through a doorway appeared Oakley. Without hesitation I ran straight over to him and flung my arms around him, dragging him into a hug.

'How very touching.'

Katherine sniggered. It took me a few seconds, but I realised suddenly he wasn't returning the hug. I pulled away and looked up at his face which was clouded with something dark. He was not resembling my friend in the way he looked at me.

'What's wrong?'

I asked and before he could respond I turned back to the abductors.

'What did you do to him?!'

I shouted, my skin tingling with anger and power. They both looked thoroughly amused with the situation but didn't reply. Instead, it was Oakley's voice that answered, and I spun back to face him.

'Do you have any idea how hard it has been to put up with your overly emotional and irritating human ways for this long?'

'W-w-what?'

My mouth dropped open. Was this some sort of ruse? I searched his face for any sign that this was part of a plan to get us out of here. Nothing. He stared at me with disdain.

'You weren't meant to have powers yet. I wasted all that time and effort getting close to you so that I could monitor you and we could move in before your powers came out, but you are certainly sneaky enough to be Fae. There's no way you have kept this secret all to yourself, so come on, who knows?'

I could hardly process what he was saying. Memories of our time getting to know each other, and building a trusting friendship, was a lie? How could he have faked that all, and why? Betrayal was not a strong enough word for how I felt.

'You're working for Katherine and Viktor?'

My voice hardly came out. They all started laughing at this.

'You think I would work for them? I serve my Queen, the rightful leader of the Unseelie realm.'

'Your queen?'

Who the hell was his Queen? I hadn't realised there was even anyone fighting for King Oberon's throne. However, he didn't answer. Instead, he dropped to one knee with his head bowed. I turned to see that the other two had done the same.

'Hello Ruby.'

A sickly sweet voice sang across the room, and out a doorway in the corner of the room appeared a female figure. She was a petite Fae with masses of raven-black hair flowing in waves down her back. It was as soon as I saw her piercing violet eyes that I realised who she was. She was just as I had seen her in that book in the library. Queen Titania.

ASH

I was making my way towards Ruby's room, wanting to explain myself more and soothe her upset over Oakley, when I heard Saffie roar. I sprinted towards the room and found Saffie in her panther form, looking absolutely distraught.

She's gone! Something is wrong!

My blood ran cold at her words.

'Where has she gone?!'

My voice thundered. The feline didn't seem fazed though, her concern remained purely with her missing companion.

I can't tell, there was another familiar here though I can smell it. One I've not encountered before. And a portal opened over there, the residue of witch magic has left a burning smell.

Katherine. She's taken her.

I thought, realisation hitting me.

We need to get to her Prince, something is wrong, I can sense it.

Saffie's panic was raising my concern even further. An audible whine came from her. The familiar had a link with Ruby which meant she could sense when something was wrong, and she was clearly sensing it now. I immediately called for Bran and demanded that he and Aoife come straight to Ruby's room. They arrived within 5 minutes, a bit breathless suggesting they had run.

'Where is she?'

Aoife's voice sounded worried as she took in mine and Saffie's distraught appearances. I hadn't realised until now how much Aoife seemed to care for Ruby.

'Katherine has taken her.'

There's no sign of a struggle, I think she went willingly.

'Why would she do that?'

Oakley. They had to be bargaining with his life to get her to go, there's no other reason she would go willingly.

Saffie sounded adamant, and I had to agree it made sense.

'Aoife, a witch portal opened over there.'

I pointed to where Saffie had indicated previously.

'I need you to find out where it went to. We need to get there as soon as possible. Bran, collect weapons and bring them back here.'

'Shouldn't we bring more of the King's guard with us?'

Bran questioned, clearing concerned over the sanity of my minimalistic approach to a hostile enemy situation.

'No. I understand the dangers are likely to be high, but

if we want to save Ruby and keep her secret protected then we need to be discreet. Need I remind you, if my father finds out, she will be dead anyway.'

I directed my last comment primarily to Aoife, aware that she was the only one who would care out of the two of them.

CHAPTER THIRTEEN

RUBY

'Titania.'

My voice squeaked. This was bad. Really bad. A million times worse than I had imagined possible.

'You're meant to be dead.'

Her giggle sounded like that of a young girl.

'Ah, so you have heard about me?'

Her childish smile would look sweet and innocent if it wasn't placed on a Fae that I knew to be incredibly old and evil.

'That's good, no introduction needed then!'

She sang, throwing her arms up theatrically. A million and one questions were fighting to escape my lips, but the pure shock was stopping me from verbalising them.

'Leave us.'

Upon her command, Viktor, Oakley, and Katherine all speedily exited the room. I could feel the trembling increasing in my body as I found myself alone with possibly the scariest creature I had met so far. The books I had read suggested she was insanely powerful... and pretty much insane all around.

'Don't be scared, we are just going to talk.'

She resumed smiling sweetly at me as she closed the distance between us. I fought the urge to run.

'You've been a difficult one to locate and get hold of Ruby. I used to have my sights firmly on you when you were a baby, but after that tragic accident with your parents and moving to various foster homes, I lost you somewhere along the way.'

'You've been stalking me since I was a baby?'

I could hardly believe it, this creature had been following me and watching me, why?

'Of course, you have something that belongs to me.'

Her smile turned to a grin now.

'This is the exciting bit! I've been hiding a portion of my powers since my supposed death, and you were my choice for holding them.'

She clapped her hands together enthusiastically.

'Hiding your powers?'

What the hell was she talking about?

'I'm a descendent of your bloodline, these are my powers.'

'Your powers? My darling, those are mine, I created you as a vessel for them until I was ready to take them back.'

'You created me as a vessel?'

Nothing was making any sense, my brain felt completely scrambled. She sighed at my lack of understanding.

'Clearly, your human side and upbringing has hindered your intelligence. Your human mother carried you for me, but you are technically my offspring. How simplified do you creatures require things? I am your mother. I seduced your human father, created you, and implanted you in your human surrogate mother. Your one purpose was to keep my powers safe for me, whilst I built my army enough and recovered enough to be ready to take back my throne.'

How would I even start processing all of this?

'Now, I am ready, that is why we have had to collect you.'

'Ready to take my powers from me?'

'My powers.' She corrected me

'What happens to me when you do that?'

She eyed me for a second, realising what I was asking.

'Well, then you can go back to your normal human life Ruby. You will have no Fae links anymore and it will be completely in the past for you. This could be the end of this absolute nightmare for you.'

Others may have believed her toothy smile and the fact that she had grabbed my hand in an attempt to look genuine. However, I was not one of those people. Her striking eyes betrayed her otherwise innocent appearance. I snatched my hand back.

'You're lying to me.' Her smile turned menacing in response

'Okay, you're not as dumb as you look. When I take my powers back, your existence is no longer needed.'

'I die.'

'Yes.'

'Then I won't let you have them.'

I shouted, backing away, eyes searching frantically for an exit. I wished at this moment I had learned how to create portals properly.

'Sweet, pathetic, human girl, I do not require your permission. Those are my powers you have and they will return to me.'

As she made her way towards me again I thrust my hand out in front of me, hoping my magic would respond. It did, and a light shot out. But to my surprise, it bounced straight off of her.

'You think you can use my own powers against me? You can't hurt me with my own magic.'

She lifted her hand and flicked it, which in turn sent my body flying and it crunched as I hit a stone pillar. I touched my head and felt the warm sticky feeling that I knew meant I was bleeding. Heat radiated from the wound. Before I could drag my body up, I was sent flying again across the floor and smacked into the wall. My ears had started ringing, but I could still hear her evil laugh in the background. Despite the now blurry vision, I could see the classic Fae portal appearing and Saffie pounced through in panther form, teeth bared and roaring. Quickly stepping to her side was the prince, with a sword in his hand, and behind them was Aoife and Bran. The Prince's eyes connected with me and scanned over my injuries, and his face turned murderously dark. They all then seemed to recognise Titania, and all but the Prince's face went rather pale.

'Titania.'

His voice was thunderous. She seemed mildly amused as she watched the scene unfold.

'What is this? Don't tell me that the supposed Prince is harbouring feelings for my little half-breed offspring? Does your father know about this most unacceptable relationship?'

She was definitely enjoying witnessing his anger rising, and he was playing into her hands exactly as she wanted.

We need to go, there's a lot of reinforcement coming.

Saffie's voice alerted us all, her ears twitching and

picking up the distant sounds we were missing. Her eyes looked pained as she gave me a meaningful and caring stare.

'You have a familiar?'

Titania's surprise was evident, and her piercing stare moved to me and looked intrigued by me.

'How is that possible?'

She shook her head and then turned back to my friends.

'I'm not interested in any of you currently, the girl stays with me though, so if you wish to survive I would leave now.'

Saffie growled fiercely before moving towards me and positioning herself defensively in front of me.

Take her and run.

Saffie ordered. It took me a minute to understand what she had said, and what was happening. But when the portal appeared behind me and I felt arms dragging me up, I realised. I realised in time to see Titania's face grow quickly wild with fury. With a high-pitched shout she flung her arms up and released a surge of energy heading straight for Saffie. It hit her body and she instantly dropped to the floor. Within a split second, I found myself pulling away from the hands gripping me and flinging my body in front of my furry friend. I felt my voice breaking as a scream burst from my chest and I unleashed the biggest blast of power that I could muster up. Titania's smug look was instantly wiped from her face as the blast sent her flying backward. I didn't get a chance to see much else as Saffie and I were dragged through the portal.

Samira kindly treated my wounds as best she could, and so I instantly went to my best friend's side as soon as I was released from triage care. To see her so lifeless and with a mask of oxygen over her swollen nose and mouth was heart-breaking.

'She will heal.'

Samira's hand touched delicately on my shoulder.

'She just needs time. That power blast must have been incredibly strong, what was it?'

I had already been warned by the Prince to keep my mouth shut, so I decided to avoid the question.

'Can I stay here with her?'

Samira's eyes portrayed her complete sympathy.

'I'm so sorry Ruby but no, she needs to rest and heal. You can come back first thing in the morning though.'

'I won't be any trouble, I will happily sit silently and sleep in the chair, you won't even know I'm here.'

I desperately protested. The idea of leaving my familiar in this state was excruciating.

Ruby, I'm fine, I need to sleep without your snoring. Please go and get rested yourself, you won't do either of us any good by not letting yourself heal up properly.

'You're awake?'

I began to sob, hearing her voice in my head again was the most comforting sound I could possibly hear at that moment.

Only because you won't shut up.

Saffie's laughter was weak.

I really don't want to leave you here Saff. I am so sorry for what happened, I didn't...

Please, Ruby, don't. It wasn't your fault, and I don't blame you. But I will blame you if you don't get your butt out of here and let me sleep.

I love you Saff, and I will be back as soon as I can tomorrow morning.

Not too early please, It will be my first peacefully quiet night since meeting you.

She managed a wink at me, and I gently hugged her, kissed her head, and left the room.

Tears were still streaming down my face as I made my way to my room, but thankfully the sobbing had subsided. The Prince made me jump as I entered the room, he was sat silently on the end of my bed and stood up the instant I stepped in.

'I'm sorry I didn't mean to scare you. I had to check you were okay.'

He seemed to notice my tears straight after he spoke, and his hand reached out quickly to stroke my cheek, his thumb wiping the moisture from it.

'The pain?'

He questioned, assuming that was the reason for my crying. I shook my head.

'Saffie.'

'How is she?'

'She looks like shit, but is still as feisty as ever.'

I managed a slight smile.

'I'm glad. And you?'

His fingers stroked my hair back, his eyes wandering over my face and neck. A strong part of me wanted this to continue, but the overwhelming exhaustion confirmed to me that I was in no mood to entertain these strange interactions that would inevitably end up leaving me more confused.

'I'm exceptionally tired and could do with a nap.'

I stepped around him and made toward my bed.

'Of course, yes. We have a lot to discuss, but it can wait until you have recovered a little from the ordeal.'

His voice was matter-of-fact but I got the distinct impression his feelings towards my dismissive response ran deeper than they looked. He left without saying another word, and I laid starfished on my bed and staring at the ceiling. It didn't take too long before I felt my eyes closing, and I willingly fell into the darkness.

My dreams had been filled with vampires and witches mostly, but the worst had been seeing Oakley with Titania's glowing violet eyes. I had awoken in a flood of my own sweat and a through-the-roof heart rate. My furry friend was still asleep when I arrived to see her, but my presence quickly woke her. She looked exhausted still, but less deathly at least.

'Saff, you look terrible.'

I laughed as I grabbed her paw.

Not looking too hot there yourself.

Her voice was weak, but her sass was still very much present which made me smile.

'I'm so sorry Saff.'

I bowed my head, unable to look at her whilst I spoke, the guilt very much eating away at me

'I never wanted anyone to get hurt, least of all you. I just couldn't let Oakley die because of me. I was offered a trade, my life for his, and I couldn't have lived with myself if I didn't accept it.'

I understand, and there is nothing to be sorry for.

Her voice was significantly more sympathetic than I had expected. I wanted to fling my arms around my best friend, but refrained out of fear that I would break something in her already fragile body. *I'm assuming they had lied, Oakley was already dead?*

'No.'

This time I managed to look up, tears stinging furiously in my eyes.

'He is one of them. Has been all this time too.'

Saffie's eyes bulged and then narrowed as she grumbled angrily.

I'll rip his throat out, the little weasel.

She growled, teeth snarling.

'I just can't believe it. I thought he was my friend.'

My lip started to tremble, threatening a full-on sob eruption.

Don't you dare.

Saffie commanded so harshly that I instantly stopped and stared.

Ruby Goodall, if you waste even one tear on that lying waste of air then I swear I will claw your pretty little face off. He has helped to cause us to be here rather than at home in the human world. He has lied to your face and built a false friendship with you. He is the reason that I am lying here like this. Do not dare cry over him.

Her words sparked a fire within me. She was right. He had lied to me. He was at least part of the cause for my entire life turning upside down, and he was the reason my best friend had nearly died. Just like that, my tears dried up and I was fuelled by an overwhelming urge for revenge. He had preyed on me in that way because he had perceived me as weak and naive.

You are right Saff. Next time I will be ready for them, and they will all get to see what I am truly capable of.

This earned a toothy smile from Saffie. I would up my efforts in developing my powers, and I would make sure that I was no longer weak.

We continued to talk from then onwards about her injuries and how she had found the night, right up until our conversation was interrupted by the entrance of the Prince, Aoife, and Bran. The prince ordered the staff in the area to take a break, so that we had some privacy, and everyone joined me around Saffie's bed.

'I'm glad you're alive Saffie.'

Aoife was the first to speak, and I don't know why but I was surprised to hear the genuine and kind comment, I hadn't realised she had any fondness for Saffie before now. Saffie nodded back to her as a way of a thank you.

'Ruby, you need to tell us what happened before we arrived yesterday?'

The Prince was quick to draw us back to the main issue at hand.

'Yes, of course.'

I stumbled over my words, trying to organise how to begin.

'Well, I was offered a trade by Katherine's familiar. My life for Oakley's.'

'And you were stupid enough to accept?!'

Aoife's voice took on a tone that I didn't think it was capable of.

'Apparently so.'

I exhaled, aware that there would be no point in explaining my all too human feelings of guilt that played a large part in that decision-making process. I continued on to explain what had happened. I had expected more than just raised eyebrows when I revealed Oakley's hidden motives and split personality, but I supposed I couldn't be surprised at the Fae for not being particularly emotive. However, emotion did strike when I revealed my link with Titania. Aoife jumped up from her chair and shouted.

'What?!'

Bran looked horrified and asked me how that was possible. Saffie yelped in worry, and the Prince just stared at me with a haunted expression.

'You're sure? She could be lying. She isn't renowned for honesty.'

Bran tried to reason. This was possibly the most he had ever spoken to me and the most concern he had ever shown for me.

'I don't know, but it does make sense in some ways. I felt as if I knew her when I was looking her up before, and I have her weird powers.'

'So what is our next move?'

Aoife asked, her brows dipped heavily into a concerned frown. The Prince thought on his answer for a minute, whilst we all waited expectantly.

'We will have to tell the King.'

No. Not a chance. Ruby will be executed.

'We don't have a choice, we need to be prepared for Titania's inevitable attack on the throne. We will keep Ruby's ties to her out of it and of course her magic progression, but the rest has to be dealt with.'

There was a silent agreement and understanding among us all.

The King appeared calm externally, but his eyes betrayed him in showing the sheer fear from hearing that Titania was still in fact alive. The prince very carefully avoided too much of my involvement. His tale of events led to Oakley and Katherine taking me hostage through the portal. It seemed plausible enough that they would follow after me, as the King would not have wanted his captive to escape.

'The girl. She is in on this, she is Titania's bloodline. Lock her up!'

He finally pointed a finger at me, deciding my guilt instantly.

'No, she was just unfortunately in the way at the time.'

The Prince tried to reason with his father. I felt a flighty feeling growing in my stomach. I wondered how far I would make it if I just ran. I desperately wished Saffie was with me at this point.

'Coincidences do not happen.'

The King's eyes squinted at me in complete distrust.

The Prince seemed to take a different approach.

'Perhaps not. But, they had no interest in her when we arrived, and were happy to kill her. They had wanted me.'

'Ah, yes.'

The King twiddled his beard, the cogs visibly turning in his brain as he thought.

'It would make sense to take the Prince of the throne, that way there will be no successor when they try to kill me. The rest of you, out!'

He yelled, waving us off. Aoife grabbed my arm and dragged me swiftly from the room.

CHAPTER FOURTEEN

RUBY

I suddenly felt very alone in my room, without Saffie. So I decided to throw on some gym clothes and make my way down to the training room to expel some energy. To my disappointment, I found that it was completely empty, so my only choice was to spar with the inanimate objects in the room. Pulling my phone out of my pocket I decided to connect it to the training room speakers and blast some enthusiastic music to get me in the mood. A bit of ACDC to start me off seemed to do the trick. Skipping a full warm up, and instead just briefly stretching my arms and thigh muscles, I began to jog on the spot with my fists clenched defensively in front of my face. It took a minute to get into it, but when I did my imagination turned the punching bag into Oakley. That disgusted look that he had the nerve to give me, his traitorous smug face, was what I focused on and immediately my body flared with anger. How dare he trick me into thinking he was my friend, all meanwhile plotting to help the crazy woman that wanted to kill me. My mind flicked to our evening under the stars.

'How could you?!'

I screamed and threw a fist as hard as I could at the bag. It wobbled slightly, and I followed it up with an upper-cut. I ducked and weaved around him, anticipating the moves that I had seen him use in the training sessions here. I continued the assault on the Oakley bag until I was struggling to breathe, and sweat was pouring off of me. Tears stung at my eyes, and I wiped at them with my now drenched top. My muscles were burning but it felt good, there was something relaxing in the adjustment to physical pain.

'I will find you and I will make you pay for this.'

I promised the Oakley bag before giving it a final punch and leaving the training room.

After a mildly revitalising shower, I laid on my bed staring at the ceiling, trying to sort through everything that was happening in my head. So much had happened in such a short space of time, and it was beginning to feel like I was becoming someone unrecognisable. But then who was I really before? Someone who had no real idea who she truly was, someone who didn't have any idea that the woman she had called mother for years was in fact not. Was my life even really mine, if all I was born to be was a vessel for Titania's powers? My hands clasped over my face, my teeth grinding together, as I tried desperately to hold in the sob that was threatening to break free. I was so tired of crying lately. But my body couldn't hold on anymore, the tears fought their way out, and the cries of emotional pain erupted. Turning over, I buried my face into the pillow hoping it would stifle some of the noise I was creating in my otherwise deadly silent room.

I must have fallen asleep at some point because a knocking on the door made my eyes peel open.

'Ruby, can I come in?'

Aoife's voice called nervously through the door. I grunted back an OK to her, and she peeked her head through to look at me before finally deciding to actually come in.

'Everything okay?'

'Why wouldn't it be Aoife?'

I groaned back sarcastically. I knew it wasn't fair to be grumpy with her, but I couldn't help myself. She tilted her head whilst observing me.

'You've been crying.'

'Really? Hadn't noticed. You would cry too if you were me. Or actually, you probably wouldn't, you lot seem to be mostly emotionally void.'

As soon as the words came out of my mouth I regretted them, but thankfully Aoife just shrugged and laughed.

'Probably true.'

'What can I do for you Aoife?'

I sighed, sitting myself up and leaning my back against the bed headboard. This was an odd sight, to see her nervous. She sat down opposite me on the bed and paused, seeming to consider her words carefully.

'I figured you may need someone to talk to, with Saffie in recovery I assumed you would probably not have anyone to confide in about everything you have been through.'

Suddenly the nerves made sense. Aoife was completely out of her comfort zone, but she was here to try and be a supportive friend to me. She had considered that I was not like them, and had come to check in on me. If I had had enough fluid left in my body I could have cried all over again at this beautiful gesture. Instead, I flung my arms around her and pulled her into a tight hug. Her body froze and went rigid in discomfort at my display of affection.

'Sorry, I forgot you lot don't do that.'

I laughed, releasing her, and thankfully she recovered from her surprise and laughed with me.

'Thank you Aoife, It honestly means so much to me that you would come here like this.'

Her genuine smile back at me was heart-warming. It was easy to see now, retrospectively, that Oakley had been faking our friendship. The Fae were not naturally open to their emotions or expressive of them. They also were not keen on anything lesser than Unseelie, and a half-breed like me was certainly considered lesser.

I don't know how long she sat patiently and listened to me ramble on for, but she did so without any sarcastic or blunt responses, and it was almost like speaking to one of human girlfriends again.

'How is any human meant to deal with all of this? We aren't made for this world.'

'You're not really human Ruby.'

This was the first time someone here had considered me not to be mostly human.

'I know you are part, but your Fae side is taking over and getting stronger. I can't begin to imagine how difficult it must be to have to adapt everything to a completely different way of life, and everything you know has been turned upside down, but this is your life now. It's time to start accepting that.'

Whilst her point in itself seemed blunt, she said it with such compassion that I couldn't be offended. She was right. As desperately as I wanted to hang on to the possibility of some sort of return to normality, it was never going to happen. It was time to embrace my new life.

A few days passed relatively peacefully, with increased training and plenty of visits to Saffie. The Prince and the king's guard had been distant, busy with planning for an expected war it seemed. I had been returning from another trip to visit Saffie, whose wit and sarcasm had certainly made a full recovery now, when I was called into the training room for a meeting. In the training room stood the Prince, Aoife, and Bran who all turned at the same time to stare at me entering. The Prince and I made eye contact briefly before he pulled his attention away, an unusual expression on his face.

'Aoife and Bran I need you to start rallying up the troops and inform them of what is going on, we need as many Fae as possible on side and ready. Ruby and I will visit the Eclipse coven to convince them to join with us against Titania.'

'What makes you think they would help us? Witches are hardly fans of the Fae, and they tend not to care about Unseelie politics.'

Bran questioned.

'Delilah and I go back a way, she owes me a favour.'

The Prince answered, sounding sure of himself.

'Plus, after Katherine's stunts on covens around the country, they will be keen to help us bring her to a stop.'

This answer seemed to satisfy Bran's questions as he simply nodded in understanding. My brain felt a little frazzled with too many questions I wanted to ask. However, I kept quiet. The Prince was clearly in a rush to act, and as such my questions would likely not be well received. Obediently I nodded along, pretending to understand.

Our portal landed outside a very large white house, surrounded by an iron gate and at least eight-foot fencing. I stifled a gasp at the impressive house. The Prince sighed as if the effort of ringing the gate's bell was too much. A sharp voice sounded over the speaker, asking who we were before admitting us inside the gate. The front garden was mostly a large span of beautifully arranged flowers and exotic-looking plants, with a cobblestone path leading up to the front door. As we approached it, the door swung open and I nervously followed behind the Prince as we entered. A gasp escaped my lips as I took in the extravagant surroundings, an oversized staircase stood in front of us, and to my right there appeared to be a living room that was the size of the whole downstairs of my house. To my left was the dining room, with a ridiculously big dining table and a million chairs surrounding it. Seated at the far end of the table was a young woman.

'Why hello there, what brings the Unseelie Prince to my door?'

She stood as we entered the dining room, a confident smile beaming across her lips and flashing her dazzling white teeth.

'Delilah.'

He nodded in response, the workings of a strained friendly smile hinting on his face.

'To what do I owe the pleasure?'

She was more assertive and confident than I would have imagined she would be when confronted by the Prince. So far, I was impressed.

'We have come to ask for your coven's assistance.'

Delilah's eyebrow raised curiously.

'It has come to our attention that Titania has risen and is currently forming an army to attempt to take over the Unseelie realm.'

'And why should that concern us witches?'

'The witch Katherine Sparrow has aligned herself with

Titania, along with some vampires. I believe you may be interested in assisting Katherine's capture so that you can punish her for her crimes against her own coven and the others she has brutally assassinated.'

'Katherine Sparrow you say.'

Delilah's gaze dropped to her hands spread on the table in front of her, her brow now creased in thought.

'I am of course aware of Katherine's crimes of late. She is of great value to us, as there are many that wish to ensure appropriate sentencing for her crimes.'

Delilah seemed to be having an internal battle with herself over the matter, though why I couldn't imagine.

'I am cautious about getting involved in your Fae affairs, especially as from what I know of Titania.'

She finally admitted. There it was, fear. So she was scared of Titania and the Fae.

'She is currently weakened and so we plan to attack whilst she is more vulnerable.'

I was so glad that he didn't mention my involvement with her powers. Delilah took a minute to stare at him before moving out from behind the table and striding towards us. Her model-like legs were sticking out of a knee-height black skirt, and the high black heels only accentuated them. In a normal world, I may have been jealous, in this situation however I was too nervous and confused to feel much else. She stood square on with the prince, clearly trying to assure him of her strength and authority. He seemed unfazed.

'Okay Prince, we will assist you.'

She nodded her head, her lips remained tight and her brow slightly frowning though, indicating a great deal of concern was escalating inside her.

'But Katherine Sparrow is ours, she is not to be killed.'

'I can promise only that we will do what we can to prevent her death and ensure a safe handover to yourself.'

'That is a very Fae promise, no certainty, and limited reassurance.'

She grumbled. The Prince shrugged, unmoving in his attitude or response.

'Fine. What do you need from us?'

She ever so slightly bowed her head in a discreet sign of submission.

'I need enough of you to take down Katherine, and her vampire associates.'

'So, we are there to take down the lesser beings for you?'

'Do you wish to take on Titania's Fae army instead?'

The Prince countered, his own sarcastic smirk competing with hers.

'Touché. I will assemble my own coven and any others that I can get on board.'

'Excellent. Tonight, bring them to the Unseelie castle.'

She looked as though she might argue with the crazily tight timeframe, but a look from the Prince made her close her mouth again.

As if noticing me for the first time since our arrival her gaze snapped onto me.

'And who is your friend?'

She made her way towards me. A tingly feeling crept over me, almost as if it were trying to probe into my skin.

'What are you?'

She asked curiously.

'This is Ruby.'

The Prince introduced me. She continued to eye me curiously, circling me like a predator.

'She's half Fae.'

'She is only a half-breed?'

Surprise lit her face.

'You are very powerful, but it's hidden. I hadn't even registered your aura here right away, but now I can feel your defences.'

Her hands raised, palms facing me she continued.

'You are a little ticking time bomb, your power is right at your seams wanting to erupt. There is a discrepancy inside you though, two sets of powers building together.'

She seemed completely lost in her analysis of me, right up until the Prince cleared his throat and brought her back into the room.

'Right, I will gather my coven and we will meet you at the castle this evening. I assume you can accommodate us for the time being?'

She snapped right out of it and turned her back to me.

'Of course. Thank you Delilah.'

His smile seemed slightly more tense compared to when we first arrived. I found myself wishing that she had continued her peculiar reading of me. Two powers? Strange. I was looking forward to seeing Saffie to discuss this. Samira should be finished with her by now.

We left the extravagant witch house and I immediately sprung on the Prince with my questions.

'What happens now then? How do you know that they can be trusted? What will they do with Katherine when they get hold of her? Do you think...'

I got cut-off part way through my string of never-ending queries as the Prince span and stood in front of me. I stumbled to a stop.

'You're worried.'

It seemed to be more of a statement than a question.

'Well, yes, of course I am.'

A nervous feeling crept over me at the close contact. He

didn't appear to notice the close proximity. I guessed Fae were not aware of personal space.

'You don't need to worry, I will not allow harm to come to you.'

His gaze intensified and a strange cooling effect tingled at my skin. I wasn't sure how I knew, but I could sense that it was the Prince's magic enveloping me in a comforting gesture. Somehow it felt more intimate than a physical embrace even. My fire magic bubbled to the surface and met his ice magic in a pleasant reaction.

ASH

The meeting of our magic was a connection that I hadn't expected to ever materialise, and I certainly hadn't expected them to conjure up further emotions towards Ruby. She didn't understand it, but I did. She hadn't been raised in the Fae world, so for her this connection would not have been something that she would have ever even considered, but for me, I had just never thought myself capable of it. I had witnessed many true matches form based on their magic. Aoife and Bran were an example of it, with their mutual earth magic. Fire and ice shouldn't have connected like that, they should have combatted for dominance. Ours, however, seemed to intertwine and strengthen one another. The connection solidified my decision and internal debate; I was in love. It was a strange concept for me to make sense of, as I had been resisting acceptance for a while now. I could tell that she had not registered it yet, and there were more pressing things for her to address before I could ask her to explore her emotions towards me. I would have to be patient, it was a virtue I generally did not possess, but this was different. This incredibly resilient woman needed me to remain focused on the task at hand and act as her support system through the upcoming challenges.

I took a step back, dragging my magic reluctantly from her, and then silently created a portal for us to leave through. Ruby remained mute as she presumably mulled over the experience internally. When we reached the other side I ordered her to find Aoife for some combat practice, and for once she complied without any sign of reluctance. I however took a deep breath and prepared to engage in updates on the witch agreement with my father.

CHAPTER FIFTEEN

RUBY

'Where the hell am I?'

My thoughts tumbled out of my mouth as I squinted in the dark to try to make out anything familiar.

'Hello again Ruby.'

A voice seemed to surround me. It took me a few seconds, but I quickly recognised that sickly voice that turned my blood cold. Titania. Also, less affectionately, known apparently as my mother. Seconds later, before I could form a response, candles flickered to life around the room. The candles illuminated the area just enough for me to make out that we were in the castle's hall. There was something different about it though, aside from the particularly unhelpful dim lighting. My eyes searched the hall, trying to determine why It seemed wrong. The portraits. What had previously been hangings of The King and The Prince, and what I had assumed were other members of the Unseelie royal family, there were instead other people's faces staring at me from the walls. Titania was featured on most of them, her eyes burning into me from all angles. But another set of eyes that stirred my curiosity was from a younger Fae man who featured in all of the backgrounds of the pictures. Something in my brain was screaming at me to remember, but before I could push my memory any further a figure in the corner of my eye had my head snapping round. Titania.

'This was what it looked like before I was betrayed and sent into years of hiding.'

Her eyes gazed around the room, a small smile playing on her lips as though she were enjoying the memory before her stare settled back onto me.

'So, daughter, how are you enjoying my powers?'

Her eyes pierced into mine, and it took everything in me to not flinch away from her stare.

'They're great thanks.'

I managed to quip back. This didn't have the intended effect though, Titania simply chuckled.

'So what is this master plan? Kidnap me and bring me to this weird replica castle?'

'You're so human. This is a dream, daughter. You are peacefully sleeping in your bedroom at the real castle, safe from harm.'

Her eyes lit up with an evil glow.

'Safe from me, for now anyway.'

'So you're invading my dreams now? Why?'

Thankfully my voice didn't tremble, and I managed to maintain eye contact with Titania, despite wanting to search desperately for an exit. Her smile returned to the sickly sweet façade, as she began to strut towards me. I wanted to back away quickly, but my feet remained planted. Her fingers reached out and stroked through the waves of my hair that framed my face.

'You remind me so much of myself.'

My choking noise of disgust clearly amused her.

'Oh I know you must find that impossible to believe, but it's true. That feisty, determined side of you, it comes from me.'

'Last time I checked, feisty and determined aren't synonyms for absolutely psychotic.'

'Psychotic is a strong word from someone who knows very little about me.'

'What more would I need to know? Let me guess, some sort of tragic childhood led you to being this way, and it's everyone else's fault?'

'I'm not sure I would call it a tragic childhood, but it certainly shaped me into who I am today.'

Her smile twisted slightly and her eyes lost a little shine. Had I hit a nerve with this topic? I knew I needed to work out how to wake up, but my curiosity was piqued too much and so I had to ask.

'In what way?'

Her eyes bored into mine as she seemed to be weighing up whether to have that conversation or not.

'Fancy a little family history lesson, do you? Before I was Queen Titania, my father ruled. He was an... interesting man.'

'Interesting in what way?'

'He was considered by the realm as a fierce, determined, and forceful leader. By his family, he was seen less favourably.'

Her smile took on a weary appearance and her eyes glazed over as she was visibly transported back in her mind. I knew this would be a perfect opportunity to try and escape or wake myself, but I was fixated on her, on the story unfolding.

'My mother was a meek, feebly quiet little woman. My parents were matched through his need for a high-standing queen to carry his children, and through her family's desire for more power and social status. My mother was expected to produce him an heir, a strong Fae male who would be able to take his place when the time came. However, he was unfortunate enough to have me, a daughter. He hated me from the minute I was announced female, and my mother suffered greatly for producing me. She didn't manage to produce any further children and eventually, she was considered to not be useful any longer.'

Her tone remained level and her face unchanged, but there was an air of sadness as she spoke.

'He killed her?'

My question surprised even me. I was too invested in her story. But then, these were technically my grandparents, wasn't it normal to be curious?

'It was swept under the carpet very quickly and my cries for my mother and questions were met with brutality that quickly taught me that silence was key to survival in that household. For years my father made it clear that I was his life's biggest disappointment, and eventually, he turned to trying to find a suitable mate for me that would be acceptable enough to take the throne in the future. I knew I couldn't have my freedom taken from me, like my mother's was, and I refused to live under the treacherous hands of another male. So, armed with that determination, and the long-brewing anger for my mother's murder, I plotted to end my father's reign and take the throne for myself.'

'You killed your father?'

My shock at this revelation was more than a little audible. She had plotted and killed her father, which in itself rang completely crazy, so did it make me crazy as well to feel a sense of understanding?

'Don't sound so surprised Ruby, you may think I'm a monster, but believe me when I say that I learned from the best.'

'How did you do it? How did you kill him?'

I couldn't explain why I wanted to know, but I desperately did want to. Her eyes seemed to zone back into the room and the intensity focused back onto me.

'And you think we aren't alike?'

I opened my mouth to protest her mocking comment, but I was quickly cut off as she continued.

'It took years of planning. The first couple of attempts were thwarted by unexpected changes, and so I learned that I had to wait for the opportune moment to find me rather than trying to rigorously plan for specific events. People can surprise you, even when you have studied them intensely for years. Just when I thought I may not get any more chances, we had a carriage ride to meet a potential suitor for me and we were ambushed. The carriage driver and two guards were killed, but so were the assailants. That left him and me alone in the woods. As he turned from me I took an axe from one of the guards and I buried It into the back of his head. I then made my way back to the castle and retold the story with a slight adjustment that made me into the lucky escapee rather than the murderer.'

'You axed your father in the head?'

I felt sick. I could understand her feelings of bitter resentment and fear for the future, but that was pure barbaric behaviour.

'I had dreamt of it being a bit more dramatic if I'm honest. I would have liked to have done a little speech about getting justice for my mother and securing my freedom, and all of that, but I had to accept the less satisfying means to an end.'

She took a moment to assess my reaction, before continuing

'You may believe it to be the actions of a crazy person, but answer me this; you know that I want you dead, do you plan to sit back and allow me to kill you? Or are you planning to fight back and kill me first?'

I hated to admit it but it had crossed my mind many times that I would need to kill her in order to save myself.

'It's not the same thing.'

Her head tilted slightly as her face took on a pensive appearance.

'Oh, but it is, dear daughter. However, I think it may be time to rethink my initial plan. You are not what I had thought you would be. You may have a lot of human attributes that are quite frankly repulsive and pathetic, but underneath that you have potential. You're so much more like me than I had imagined you could be. So, I am going to offer you the chance to not only survive this little power dilemma we have, but also to join me in taking back our family's rightful place on the throne.'

'You must be joking right? You think that I would trust you? And you think that I would betray the Prince and all of my friends? You really are mad!'

'The trouble with you Ruby is that you are very naïve. You think that I am the only threat to you, and you are very wrong. You are blindly ignoring the threats you live with currently.'

She laughed and shook her head mockingly.

'What do you mean by that?'

'You really think that the King is just letting a descendant of his enemy live within the castle walls without a plan in mind for you? He will gladly see you dead, there will never be any form of acceptance there for you. You are my bloodline, you are the enemy, and they will turn on you the second they can.'

'And you expect me to believe that you care or have any good intentions towards me?'

'Oh no, of course not. I may not care, but you do hold enough interest for me to want you alive and I can offer you a place at my side.'

'Oakley, was that your plan?'

I hadn't even thought the question through before it burst from my lips

'Excuse me?'

'Oakley. The befriending me and betraying me game, was that your doing?'

She clapped her hands together excitedly.

'Oh yes! Everyone had orders to find you and bring you to me, I didn't care how they went about it.'

'So it was his choice?'

A very small part had hoped that he had been forced. That hope died instantly. Like a switch, the giggling school-girl persona evaporated and her tone turned serious again.

'Oh completely. The boy has a real vendetta for the King, it's quite amusing actually, and useful too. The King and the Prince will lie to you in order to achieve what they want, I will not. You don't have to answer yet, go back with open eyes and see for yourself.'

With that, the room went dark and suddenly I sat bolt upright in my bed, gasping for breath, my eyes searching the room for Titania, who of course wasn't there.

CHAPTER SIXTEEN

RUBY

Saffie. I needed to find Saffie. My eyes scanned the darkened room and I breathed a sigh of relief as I caught sight of her curled up at the end corner of my bed. As if sensing my distress her golden saucer eyes flickered open and a sense of calm washed over me. I opened my mouth to speak, but a paranoid feeling crept through the calm and I closed it again, deciding instead to speak through our private mind link to prevent anyone from eavesdropping.

Saff, we have a problem.

With that she was up on her feet and standing to attention, urging me to explain.

Titania ambushed me in my dream.

She entered your dream? She must be getting more powerful, that sort of magic requires strong Fae powers.

But I thought she needed my powers in order to get stronger? How can she be doing it without them?

I don't know, but we need to find out.

Come on we need to tell the Prince

No, we can't.

I chewed my bottom lip uncomfortably. It didn't sit well with me to hide this from him, but Titania's warnings about the King were spinning around my head.

Why not?

Saffie pressed, her concern growing with each passing second.

Titania told me something and I need to be careful not to alert anyone of my suspicions.

Ruby, you can't seriously be trusting Titania's words?

No, of course, I don't generally, but what if she is right?

What was it she said?

She said that they will turn on me for who I am, or more who I come from as soon as I have served my purpose.

Hmm, I had suspected as such myself to be honest. The Fae are a cunning species and power means everything to them.

Well nice of you to warn me! You don't think that is why the Prince is helping me to develop my magic, do you? So he can find out what my capabilities are?

No. No, I don't think that is his intention. However, we should be cautious.

What do we do?

I trusted Saffie with my life, and in this case of not knowing what to do, I needed my best friend to advise me.

So, you're right, let's keep this to ourselves for the moment until we can establish the next best step. In the meantime, I will try to find a little solution to the dream-invading issue. With her powers growing we can't take any risks, so we need to prevent her from accessing you in that way.

I couldn't go back to sleep after all of that, and so Saffie stayed awake with me to keep me company. We chatted initially about a plan of action, and then moved on to less serious chit-chat. By the time daylight was streaming through the breaks in the curtains, my tension had eased significantly. Saffie had suggested that it would arouse less suspicion if I continued to play the ignorant part, whilst she tried digging deeper. With me pretending to be in the dark completely, Saffie should go unnoticed as she lurked around listening in where she could. We both knew time was of the essence, but so was subtlety. As normal we both attended breakfast together, and whilst I kept my head down to prevent my suspicious glances from alerting anyone, Saffie needed a couple of nudges to stop her from analysing everyone constantly. She was the furthest thing from subtle. She sat silently but looked ready to pounce at any second. Thankfully the majority of the Fae in the room were too self-absorbed to consider us worth even a glance. Except, that is, the Prince. He kept glancing in our direction during his announcements.

'Delilah, head witch of the Eclipse coven, has of course joined us and at present, they are working on location spells, and trying to break through Katherine's barriers that are hiding the perpetrators. Once we have this information it is simple, we will attack.'

'We are leading the attack on them?'

Someone asked from across the table.

'Yes. We will not wait for them to gather their resources. They will likely know the minute their protective spells are broken, and so we must strike before they have too much opportunity to prepare.'

The Prince took a second to look briefly at each person at the table.

'With this in mind, you will all need to be ready to go at any moment. There will inevitably be fatalities, but I shouldn't need to remind everyone here that the throne is what we serve. Titania and her army must be stopped, or the Unseelie realm will risk falling under her reign once again.'

I braved a look around the table myself at this point. There was an overwhelming sense of pride and determination from each of them. It was clear that each one was ready and willing to fight to their death for their realm. It was both amazing and terrifying. A silence ensued as everyone continued to eat or just sit with a thoughtful expression until we were finally dismissed.

Aoife grabbed my arm and pulled me to one side as we exited the dining room. Saffie was immediately by my side, releasing a low rumble of warning. She was definitely as on edge as me.

'What are you doing?'

I asked, perhaps sounding a little too nervous.

'We need to talk. What is going on?'

She murmured to me whilst nodding and smiling politely at the other Fae walking past. Eventually, we appeared to be alone and she returned her attention to me.

'What do you mean?'

If I hadn't sounded nervous before, then I definitely did now. Saffie edged even closer so that her shoulder fur was touching my leg.

'Don't play human.'

She pressed.

'I... I'm not. Honestly Aoife I have no idea what you are asking me.'

'What happened at the Eclipse coven residence?'

She hissed, impatience clear in her tone.

'The Eclipse place?'

Now my confusion was real. That was not what I had

expected. I wracked my brain to determine what she could mean. I felt Saffie's eyes probing me, questioning too. A couple more people wandered past and Aoife suddenly seemed uncertain, she shifted ever so slightly uncomfortably. I had seemingly gotten good at picking up on the incredibly subtle signs that the Fae showed.

'Right, my room, now.'

She whispered to us and then quickly sped off. With only a minor hesitation, Saffie and I swiftly followed.

I hesitated a little more before entering Aoife's room. She was pacing when I entered.

'Shut the door!'

She hissed nervously at me. I could sense Saffie's discomfort next to me. Something was very strange here. Aoife was never nervous like this.

'Aoife, just tell me what it is that you think I have done, you're scaring me now.'

I asked, palms upwards in a submissive position.

'The Prince. What happened with the Prince when you visited the Eclipse coven?'

I frowned, thinking back.

'We went in, we met with Delilah and the Prince talked with her about why she should help us. She wasn't sure at first, but...'

'Ruby, for the love of all that is Fae, what happened between you and the Prince?!'

She interrupted, very frustrated by this point. Suddenly the memory of that strange interaction of our powers came back to me. Surely she wasn't on about that though.

'There! That! You know what it is I'm talking about!'

She pointed her finger at me, way more animated than I had seen her behave before.

'Calm down, it was just... I don't even know how to

explain it. Our powers just seemed to interact or something like that.'

Your powers and his powers... together?

'Yes. His powers seemed to coax mine out a bit, and then they just...'

I struggled to find any words to describe it.

'They just responded to each other in a nice way. I can't explain it.'

Their faces were not what I had imagined. Shock and horror would probably best describe it.

Aoife slumped down onto her sofa.

'It's too late. She's as good as dead.'

Like hell she is! We will find a way out of this mess.

'What on earth are you two on about? Why am I dead?!'

'I warned you both that this could not continue to build between you. If I can sense it then it will soon enough be noticeable for everyone else. The King will have you killed.'

'What have I done?! I don't understand!'

My volume raised significantly.

'You really don't understand?'

She peered at me between her fingers that were covering her face. Sighing presumably at my naivety she continued

'In Fae, it is a connection so deep, our magic is bonded to our souls and so when it bonds with another they become a part of us. When it happens, there is no one else, your heart is complete and it is a once in a lifetime opportunity that most do not get. Your magic bonding with the Prince's in that way shows that you have found your love.'

'Love? Steady on, that might be a little far!'

My cheeks instantly flushed and I was audibly flustered. That was ridiculous. I couldn't be in love with the Prince. Aside from the whole initially hating him thing, and the abduction, how could I be in love with him? Sure, he was the most attractive person I had ever seen in my entire life, and I acted like a complete idiot around him, and he made me feel safe in his presence regardless of the dangers... No. This was not happening, not even an option.

'You can deny it, it won't change anything. You are linked now and the feelings will just grow.'

Aoife's resignation was alarming.

'But I don't want this, I never wanted anything like this! As if finding out I'm not even human isn't enough, I am also some evil Queen's daughter, I'm a human-shaped power vessel, and now I'm linked with the Prince forever? You have to be joking?! No. No way. I quit! I quit this crap and everything it entails!'

'Ruby...'

Aoife stood.

'No! Don't Ruby me!'

Tears were flowing excessively now and my voice became quiet as I bowed my head

'I don't want to die. I didn't ask for any of this!'

You didn't, and it is undeniably unfair. However, you will get through this Ruby, you are the strongest person I have ever met and these things will not defeat you. I will be by your side the whole way through.

I felt her wrap around my leg in an embracing gesture.

'I will be too.'

Aoife added in, surprising me.

After a few moments in silence, Saffie unwrapped herself from around my leg. Saffie and I agreed discreetly in that moment to fill Aoife in on my dream problems.

Right, we must move quickly. I will go and see what I can find out, you two will need to continue on as normal so

that we do not arouse any suspicions. Who knows who can be trusted around here.

'I think it best you stay as far away from the Prince as you can without it looking odd. I will stick by your side and try to intercept anything that may raise questions.'

'Are you not scared of helping me? Isn't that majorly against your duties to the King?'

I asked, suddenly aware of how much danger Aoife was putting herself in once again.

'Oh absolutely. If I am caught conspiring to hide this information from the King then he will make me wish for death. But I already agreed to that risk when the Prince involved me previously with your secrets. So what is one more nail in my coffin?'

A simple thank you did not seem enough for what Aoife was risking to help me, but it was all I could give.

SAFFIE

My job for the day now was simple, but the execution was likely to be anything but. My fear for Ruby, and my overwhelming responsibility to protect her, made sure that I knew I could not fail in my task. Staying in my smaller form was essential if I were to stand any chance of not being noticed. Prior to Ruby's revelation this morning, I had already utilised previous mornings to establish where the key players spent their days at various times during the day. I knew from this that the King would be in the study with his chief advisor. The door was closed but that would not matter to my superior feline hearing. Positioning myself outside of the door I listened in, whilst half-heartedly grooming myself to prevent suspicion should anyone happen to go past.

'There has been gossip of her being in the north of the realm, which would make sense as she has more supporters in that direction sire.'

The weedy brown-noser advisor's voice shook as he spoke. I had sensed he was a wimpy, wet Fae from the start. He was all talk with theory and planning, I couldn't smell an ounce of bravery on him. In fact, he seemed likely to be more use as a toothpick for my panther form than anything else.

'If that is so, then we need more men scouring up that direction for her, we need to find her if we want to stand a chance of being a step ahead of her. The Eclipse coven are taking too long with their useless witchcraft.'

The King's authoritative voice was loud and clear. I could easily assume they were talking of Titania

'Yes sire, that is a most sensible plan.'

I couldn't help but roll my eyes. Arse licker.

'I will inform the Prince so that he can assemble the correct individuals for the job.'

'See that you do. What of the plans for the half-breed?'

My ears pricked up at this, there was only one half-breed that they could be talking about.

'Everything is going to plan Sire. I have deployed the agent to obtain the spell you require and its ingredients, my King.'

'Excellent, see that he is brought to me immediately upon his return.'

'Of course Sire.'

'And I want it handled discreetly, he is not to be seen by anyone.'

'I will personally see to it.'

This couldn't be good. They swiftly moved on to discussions over the realm's finances and politics, and so I took my leave from my eavesdropping post and made my way to the library. My heart was starting to race, something awful was in motion, I could sense it. One thing was certain though, I would not allow them to hurt Ruby.

The librarian's assistant was in there today, she was an unbearably smug and self-righteous woman, and I had to grit my teeth to force a sort of friendly smile at her.

'Can I help you?'

Her shrill voice sounded as she looked down at me, her glasses gradually sliding down her long nose.

I'm looking for a sleeping spell, to improve one's sleep and keep the night terrors away.

I didn't want to give anything away, but needed pointing in the right direction if I were to stand any chance of finding something suitable.

'Your master is struggling to sleep I presume?'

She probed. The instinct to hiss at her for referring to Ruby as my 'master' was overwhelming, but I swallowed it down. Whilst it was normal for familiars to have a 'master', Ruby and I considered our relationship a friendship built on mutual respect and trust, not ownership or dictatorship. That, and I was never going to be anyone's servant. But, we currently both had our parts to play for appearances, and this was one of those times I needed to swallow my pride and accept my role in order to achieve the end goal. I showed a toothy smile, and nodded. "Follow me then" She instructed, before spinning on her heel and heading off through the stacks of books. I followed behind her, trying not to feel irritated by the echoing clicking of her heels on the wooden flooring. We eventually stopped in a section, and she announced that we had arrived.

'Do you need me to select the books from the shelves for you?'

She asked, a mocking tone evident.

Yes please, if you would be so kind.

My own responses were making me nauseous, I wanted to rip the throat out of the creature, but I was instead playing nicely with her. She smugly selected out a book on sleeping spells and placed it on the ground for me.

'I suppose you will need me to turn the pages for you too.'

Actually, I think I can manage from here thank you.

I replied, using my claw to flip the cover open. She raised an eyebrow and tutted before swanning off.

I must have been pacing the room for a good hour before Ruby returned, sweat dripping from her forehead and the forming of bruising appearing under her left eye. She clearly noticed my staring at it as she made her way over to her mirror and hissed painfully, her fingers brushing the spreading purple.

Sophie played hardball today. I think she may have enjoyed kicking my arse a bit too much.

Since when did Sophie manage to kick your arse of late?

Since my mind has been distracted with thoughts of being assassinated by the King and dreams invaded by Titania.

Yes, well, I have news on the King front.

I hated having to create that look of stress and fear on her face, the one that made her look too innocent for this life.

The King has someone searching for a spell of some sort, I don't know what it is, but I can't imagine its for anything good.

No, I don't suppose it would be.

She chewed her lip as she thought.

I will find out though Ruby, trust me.

This seemed to relax her a little. I was glad that she trusted me so much, though it did make me feel even more desperate to get to the bottom of this, as the thought of letting her down was unbearable.

In the meantime, I did manage to obtain a spell for keeping Titania out of your dreams.

Really?!

The relief in Ruby's voice was evident, and I nodded, happy that I had managed to help her in some way.

CHAPTER SEVENTEEN

RUBY

As we sat around the strategy table, Saffie on my left and Aoife on my right, I couldn't help but yawn which elicited some eye rolls and even a brave tut from someone. The sleeping potion that Saffie had prepared for me had certainly kept Titania out, but a side effect seemed to be a reluctance to stay awake. Saffie lightly growled at the tutter, in warning. The Prince gave me a slightly concerned look very briefly before resuming his cold poker face and addressing the whole of the king's guard. This would normally be the point that I would switch off, but I was acutely aware that if I zoned out I would likely fall asleep, therefore I forced myself to tune into his voice.

'We have received notice that there is an ogre out of control and terrorising the villages north of the realm. Aoife, you will need to form a team to go and eliminate the threat as soon as this meeting is over.'

'Of course my Prince.'

She nodded obediently, before giving a stern look to the rest of the group.

'Ernest and Priscilla, you can get your armour on and meet me out the front of the castle after the meeting.'

She ordered before taking another bite of her croissant. It was unusual to see Aoife eating at a meeting. Even humans didn't tend to be that unprofessional. I stashed the question away in my mind to approach her at a later date.

'Sire, I hope I'm not speaking out of turn here, but with all that is going on can we really afford to lose some of our guards for a trivial matter like an ogre?'

Sophie questioned from the end of the table. Her voice still irritated me.

'In truth, it is not ideal, no. However, there are a lot of innocent Fae dying as a result of this ogre whilst we sit safely in the castle waiting for a confirmed location.'

The Prince's tone shut Sophie up instantly and she simply nodded understanding.

'Besides, one ogre is hardly going to take long. I'm sure they will return before we even have any news.'

'Can I join them?'

My voice sounded much more pathetic than I had intended it to. I ignored Sophie's smirk. The Prince answered before Aoife could.

'No.'

'Why not?'

My question came out before I could think it through, but despite the disapproving look from him, I wouldn't back down now.

'Because it requires experienced Fae to handle an ogre situation.'

His voice portrayed the displeasure of being questioned in such a way, but there was no way I was letting this go. I needed to have an opportunity to experience more real-life combat, the training room would not prepare me for what was likely to come in my future.

'Exactly, what better way for me to learn than to watch experience at work!'

His cold stare turned onto me and he didn't say a word. It was certainly a threatening look, one that would make most people recoil. I was not one of those people though.

'I need to be prepared for what is coming, and as lovely as the training room is, it's not exactly a good representation of real life fighting situations.'

I had him there, his silence was proving that. I maintained eye contact, showing him that I was going to be stubborn about this. The eye contact started to flare up that familiar warming sensation of my powers awakening.

'I am happy to supervise her on this little excursion. With Ernest and Priscilla present, I should be able to take a back seat and do some real-life training with Ruby.'

Aoife leaned forward instantly blocking my view of the Prince, and quietening my powers into a slumber again. I felt my face redden and I quickly glanced around to check that no one had witnessed my strange connection with the Prince. Luckily it seemed they were oblivious, and I silently thanked Aoife for stepping in. I could practically feel the heat from the Prince's glare at Aoife. But, I could only respect Aoife for not shrinking back from him. Eventually, he gave a very reluctant and stiff nod.

You can't Ruby! North of the realm there is suddenly an ogre outbreak? We know Titania has been spotted north of the realm, this may not be a coincidence?! Saffie growled loudly in my head, through our private link.

Saff, why on earth would she be releasing an ogre so far

off? It would make no sense. There would be no reason for her to assume I would be there.

Well, I will be coming with you, my gut says something is wrong here.

Aoife cleared her throat and brought us back into the room. There were some sceptical expressions, and even a couple of glares.

The rest of the meeting was done quickly and with complete silence from everyone except the very icy Prince. As the group filed out of the room, I hung back to speak to him. Saffie looked deeply unimpressed and strutted out of the room. I waited until the door had firmly shut and there was no one else around before speaking.

'I know what's happening. With us, I mean.'

'Oh? And what is that?'

A very faint smirk crept along his lips, and his eyebrow raised in a challenge for me to admit it aloud.

'I know we are... connected now through our magic and souls.'

The embarrassment was unreal as I felt like a teenager professing her love to her first crush. The words sounded ridiculous, how had Aoife made it sound so normal? The Prince didn't respond, but he was carefully watching me.

'I don't really understand it yet, but there is so much going on and I don't think I can cope with figuring it out on top of everything else currently.'

'I understand that. The risks are too high at the moment for all of us, and there is a lot that needs to be sorted out. Our time will come for us to explore this new dynamic between us, but for now, all you need to know is that I am by your side. I may not always appear to be, because I need to be cautious of appearances, but you are now the most important person in my life and I will do anything to protect you.'

The words themselves and his expression were nothing short of completely genuine. I could feel the emotion behind them, and my heart fluttered with an overwhelming urge to embrace him. But, I didn't. I swallowed it down and tried to re-focus.

'Please be careful and do not engage with the ogre.'

The Prince appeared almost vulnerable.

'I will be careful. But I need actual experience if I am going to stand any sort of chance against Titania.'

'You won't be going anywhere near her.'

His voice rumbled in a low growl.

'None of us know how this will play out, and I just want to be prepared. Saffie is coming too, so I will be as safe as I can be.'

He begrudgingly nodded at me.

By the time I made it out to the front of the castle, Aoife and the others were waiting and looking impatient.

'I wonder how many people died whilst we had to wait here for you?'

Ernest muttered, earning a warning scowl from Aoife.

We took a portal to the village of Elderrott, which was apparently where the Ogre had last been sighted. Coming out the other end of the portal, we all had our weapons poised, and Saffie was glued to my side with her teeth bared. My heart was thumping as I anticipated coming face to face with the beast as soon as we exited the portal. However, we were met with a destroyed village, and a lot of shaken up Fae villagers. My mouth dropped open as I took in the Fae villagers running with buckets of water to put out still existing fires. Most of the houses were completely knocked down and ruined. Bodies lay strewn across the path, and many more injured people staggered around trying to find safety. I had never seen horrors like this, and I was sure the images would remain burned in my mind forever. My ears were ringing with the sounds of shrieking and crying surrounding us. I was pretty sure that it was part of an ear that I stepped over, but I refused to look properly for fear that I wouldn't cope any longer.

'Where is it?'

Aoife grabbed a man's arm. He stared at her hand gripping his arm for a moment before looking up and answering.

'It ran off into the forest. It destroyed our home... we have nothing.'

He held a shaky finger up and pointed off to the trees ahead. The man looked in a state of both shock and complete devastation. Blood was trickling down the side of his face, indicating he had some form of head injury too.

Aoife nodded her head, her face unmoved, and signalled for us to follow her as she stormed onwards. I sprinted up to her side.

'Wait, Aoife, we can't just leave them like this.'

'We have a mission Ruby.'

She responded, continuing on her path as I scurried to keep up.

'But look at them! Aoife stop!'

I grabbed at her arm, and this made her halt. She held my gaze in a way that made me suddenly feel very small and infantile.

'There is an Ogre on the loose, our mission is to stop it. The longer we leave it roaming, the more villages end up like this one, and the more Fae die. One key lesson you need to learn is that it is your job to see the bigger picture. If you ever hope to survive in our world, then you need to think and act like a Fae warrior, not a weak little human. This is life or death for more than just a few people here in this village.'

Her words shook me. It was not my friend looking back at me right now, but a high ranking member of the King's guard who was on a mission, and one she would not allow to fail. I nodded my compliance and fell back behind her and in line with Saffie.

Are you okay?

Saffie asked gently. I nodded rather than responding, as my emotions were too high. Thankfully Saffie understood and resumed her quick pace next to me. Marching into the forest it was a very obvious route as the ogre's size and stature had ensured that a path of destruction was left for us to follow. As we got deeper into the forest, Aoife signalled for us all to stop and be silent. I could only hear a faint noise, but Aoife seemed certain and so then signalled for us to continue on. As we drew nearer to where the noise was coming from, it became a more clear snorting and crunching harmony. Aoife signalled for Ernest and Priscilla to head off to the right, and for me and Saffie to follow her to the left. The Ogre came into sight as we circled around to attack from either side of it. I suddenly realised what the crunching noise was as I saw it finishing off a leg and spitting out a shoe. I felt the bile rise in my stomach. Oh god. Trying desperately to hold down my sick and prevent myself from passing out, I focused on Aoife and following her footsteps. I matched her exact footwork, and refused to look back over at the beast, though the noises were harder to ignore.

Eventually we stopped and I realised we were in position. This was it. I forced myself to look up, and thankfully there were no more body parts being consumed, but the ogre sat there snorting and licking its lips. In the distance, on the other side of the beast, I saw Ernest and Priscilla also getting into position. They were almost ready to attack on Aoife's command when a loud snapping noise echoed through the trees from their direction. One of them must have stepped on some of the broken branches we had seen scattered. The look of horror on Priscilla's face was instant. The ogre stood up instantly and roared a deathly scream before spotting the other two.

They've blown their cover!

Saffie's voice alarmed in my head.

'Attack!'

Aoife screamed, causing the beast to turn around to look at us, and giving Priscilla and Ernest the opportunity to attack the beast from behind.

'Stay here Ruby.'

Aoife quickly ordered before running at the creature, sword poised for attack.

CHAPTER EIGHTEEN

ASH

Delilah winked at me as she and her coven entered the room, joining the meeting. Her sickly sweet citrus perfume made my nose twitch. She stroked her fingers across the table, until she found her seat. Her chest pushed forward between her elbows as she supported her chin on her hands. I could only assume she had intended it to be a light flirtatious move, but my mind barely registered her existence as it anxiously obsessed over Ruby. There had been no news since she had left for the mission with Aoife, which could be a good sign, or a terrible one. The logical part of me was aware that there had not been enough time passed to develop justifiable concern, however logic was not in control of my new and unfamiliar emotional side. I had wanted to leave the table, through a portal, and go straight to find Ruby. That, however, would have been a grave mistake, and so I fought off the urge and remained following my duties. I was, on the other hand, happy that Ruby was out of the way now that Delilah and her coven had broken through Katherine's warding spells and identified a location.

'We have received updates on Titania's whereabouts and it is essential we are ready to strike before her resources strengthen any further. The Eclipse coven have at last managed to locate the witch Katherine and this is where we believe Titania and her army to be also.'

The King announced to the group, ensuring that everyone's attention was fully captured. He then turned his gaze to me, an indication that it was my turn to take over. As head of the King's guard, it was my duty to provide an expertly devised plan of attack, which by chance happened to be something I was particularly skilled at. Whilst nepotism may have secured my title, there was also no doubt in my mind that I would have been selected for it regardless of my heritage.

'Based on the intel we have...'

I began, arms folded and regarding each attendee with eye contact. I took a breath to continue, but before the words left my mouth the door slammed open and a head rolled fiercely towards us, stopping just shy of my feet. The lifeless eyes of Clem stared up at me. I never had been keen on him.

'I'm afraid the intel may have been a little behind the times.'

Katherine laughed as she swanned in through the door threshold and made a theatrical hand gesture.

'Ignis!'

A shout from behind me bellowed. A flame licked at Katherine's feet, but with a swish of her hand, they were gone. In return, the young witch that had flung the spell began screaming, and as I turned I managed to catch the look of agony before she burst into dust.

'Really Delilah? Some half-wit newbies are expected to stop me?'

Katherine's laugh grew louder as she desperately aimed to flex her powers.

'Titania has given me more power than you and your pathetic little coven can even imagine.'

It was then that I heard the cries of battle occurring outside, and possibly within the castle. The king's guard were defending against an army. Titania's army to be precise. So where was Titania? As the thought occurred to me, Katherine's attention flew to me.

'In case you're wondering, Prince, the Queen is on her way to find her daughter. That Ogre was my idea.'

The smug look on her face set my blood to boil, and a murderous rage took over as I realised that Ruby was in trouble. I briefly heard my father gasp at the revelation of Ruby's tie to Titania. Before I could stop myself, I had withdrawn my sword and attacked. I took her by surprise, but I couldn't cross the room quick enough for it to stop her from sending me tumbling backward with her magic. Leon speedily hurried the King off to the side door to get him to safety. Delilah instantly threw a heavy dose of magic back at Katherine, causing her to just stumble a few steps. This was not going to be an easy defeat, but I needed to hurry if I were to get to Ruby in time.

RUBY

I watched, eyes so wide they felt close to popping out of their sockets, as the ogre raised its giant fist and sent it crashing down toward Aoife. She managed to narrowly avoid being crushed as she dropped and rolled to the left.

Priscilla swung her sword at the beast's leg and caused it to let out a deafening shout. With that, it flung its arm at her and a stomach-turning crunch sounded as it connected with her and sent her flying. Her body lay motionless against the rock the beast had previously been leaning on. Ernest and Aoife didn't pause to look though, they moved in again, swords swinging. They managed to strike it on either side and avoid the flailing limbs. The damage seemed to be very minimal considering the hits that it had taken. Priscilla had seemingly gotten it good before she was attacked back, but the beast was acting as though it had been nothing more than a little scratch. My stomach began twisting in a nervous and instinctual way, something was wrong.

'It's not going down!'

Ernest yelled to Aoife. The concern and confusion on both of their faces was obvious. They continued attacking and dodging, but the beast was still standing and fighting back.

Something isn't right. I think the Ogre is spelled, it shouldn't be able to withstand all of that.

Saffie fidgeted as she observed the scene ahead.

Spelled? Like by a witch?

Precisely.

I tore my eyes away from the battle scene ahead and looked straight into my best friend's eyes.

Katherine?

I asked, hoping desperately she would say no. Her silent stare confirmed to me that she thought the same.

That means this is a trap.

We need to get you out of here.

It was then that I heard a shout and another loud crunch, I turned my head just in time to see Ernest being flung into the bushes he had previously hidden in. Aoife was standing alone against the beast. Her chest was heaving up and down heavily, she was clearly exhausted. The ogre swung at her and she only just managed to move herself out of the way, but he did catch her blade, and sent it careering through the trees.

Aoife needs us!

Ruby don't!

I heard Saffie's words, but my body was moving out into the opening and toward the scene before I could even register them. It was only when the ogre turned its attention to me that I realised how stupid I had been. I withdrew my sword, and within a flash, Saffie was by my side roaring at the beast.

If I die because of you, I will haunt you.

Saffie warned, winked at me, and then lunged at the creature. Her teeth clamped onto its leg quickly, and before it could swipe at her, she had swiftly moved to the back of it and raked her claws down it. More screams. Aoife had pulled out some daggers from her belt, and was also running in and slashing with fury, her energy clearly renewed. I sucked in a deep breath as my friends worked their arses off to bring down the ogre. Time to do my part. I had wanted real-life training, and this was it.

Following Aoife's cues, I lunged towards the left hand side of the beast and hacked into its fleshy thigh. Aoife, Saffie, and I moved around each other as though we had practiced and prepared for months, like dancers performing a final show. My sword was dripping green sludge, which I could only assume was the monster's blood. Despite our efforts, and the fact the ogre looked like a sieve from all the stab wounds, it still hadn't succumbed to the injuries.

'How do we kill this thing?!'

I screamed, hoping my companions had some sort of

plan, as my chest was beginning to burn from the over-exertion.

We need to break the spell, but without the witch here I don't know how we can

Even Saffie's internal voice sounded exhausted. We were at risk of being wiped out in this state.

'Ruby, boost me!'

Aoife yelled and I managed to dip to my knee just in time to catch Aoife's foot as she ran and jumped towards me. With the last of my strength, I threw her upwards further and watched in amazement as she plunged her long knife straight into the beast's eye. Landing like an absolute ninja, she yelled.

'Move!'

Saffie and I speedily moved out of the way as the creature let out one final roar and at last fell down in death.

'How on earth did you know that would work?'

I asked, breathless and incredulous.

'I didn't.'

'Seriously?!'

'Yes. But call it an educated guess. I made an assumption that the brain was the part affected by the spell, considering the ogre was bleeding and capable of sustaining injuries that didn't self-heal. Therefore, going through the eye and into the brain seemed like a good final try.'

I'm impressed.

I looked at my friends, struggling for breath and covered in a mixture of blood, sweat, and ogre sludge.

'Oh God, the others!'

I quickly jumped to my feet. Saffie and Aoife exchanged a look, before Saffie's anguished eyes came back to me.

They're gone Ruby.

'You don't know that!'

I ignored their look of sympathy, and hurried over to Priscilla. Her crumpled body looked broken and crushed in the rib area. Moving the hair from her face, I could see her grey complexion. Placing my fingers on her neck confirmed what the image in front of me suggested, she was dead. Standing back up, I ran to the bushes where Ernest had been thrown. I found him in a similar state, and again with no pulse. I felt the tears stinging my eyes. I hadn't known them well, as they were relatively quiet and experienced members of the King's guard, but I felt the loss. They had fought hard and this wasn't a fair outcome.

I made my way back over to Aoife and Saffie.

'We need to get back, and have our injuries looked at.'

'Injuries?'

I mumbled under my breath. I suddenly noticed the bruising forming on Aoife's face, and looked down at my own legs to see my trousers had been torn and blood was seeping through. I guess the adrenaline had prevented me from feeling it. I nodded, sighing with a sudden over-whelming exhaustion. Things were starting to hurt now as I began the come down from it all.

We need to hurry up and get away from here, this was definitely a planned attack.

Saffie's alarmed voice also warned us. Just as Aoife was standing and getting ready to open a portal, a familiar voice spoke from behind us.

'Nice work dream team.'

It took me all of a couple of seconds to recognise it. My blood ran cold instantly as I spun round and came face to face with Titania. Aoife immediately drew her knife and launched it at our enemy. The knife paused just before Titania's face, and that classic evil smirk of hers formed just before the knife spun around and came flying back at us. The knife pierced through Aoife's shoulder and pinned her to the tree. Before she could rip it out, another came out of nowhere and secured her other shoulder into place. Her face went white as she stared past me, quickly following her line of vision I managed to turn in time to witness Saffie launching at herself at Titania. I tried to scream but my body and voice had frozen in fear as I watched Titania swipe her hand at my best friend, as though swatting a fly. I heard a hideous crunch as Saffie's body wrapped around a tree and fell limp to the floor. I managed to take a step, starting to sprint over to her, when a cold hand wrapped around my arm and dragged me through a portal. As I went through the last thing I saw was the Prince appearing through his own portal, his eyes wide and feral as he witnessed my abduction. I heard him roar my name, and then I was gone.

CHAPTER NINETEEN

RUBY

'Where are we?'

I asked, taking note of the dark, gloomy surroundings. It had been daylight when we went through the portal, but I appeared to have stepped into the night's darkness. The trees shrouded against the moonlight that was trying to break through to us, their branches reaching across to one another in a conspiratory effort. The silence was deafening. Every instinct was screaming at me to run, that this place was dangerous. With the threat of my current environment, I momentarily forgot about Titania and the threat she posed.

'They call it the dead forest.'

Her voice sounded softer than before, but that underlying poisonous nature was still evident.

'Why is it called that?'

Why would I ask that? It very clearly wasn't going to be a comforting answer. I internally scolded myself for speaking before thinking.

'Because everything dies here. It's a game of predator and prey, hunt and be hunted, fight for survival.'

A slight dramatic tone seeped back in as she seemingly got excited at the sickening prospect. Absolute lunatic.

'So you've brought me here to kill me?'

It was more of a statement than a question, as there could be no other reason for taking me to somewhere known for killing people. She cocked her head, seemingly analysing me. That sadistic smile crept along her lips again.

'No Ruby, I haven't brought you here to kill you.'

She paused momentarily as if in thought.

'Well, not unless you answer incorrectly I suppose.'

She attempted a sickeningly sweet smile, and my hatred for her bubbled even further.

'Aoife and Saffie...'

I managed their names before she lifted a hand to hush me.

'Not a concern you need to worry about currently. You decided to ban me from your dream world, and so I had to take other measures to ensure that I could contact you.'

'So violence and abduction seemed a more reasonable choice than say a text or phone call? I'd even settle for carrier pigeon!'

My voice had reached a level that definitely did not hide my sheer panic. This seemed to please her.

'Have you thought on my offer, dear daughter?'

Her use of the term 'daughter' made me feel physically sick. To know that I was related to this monster was unfathomable.

'I have.'

'And what is your choice?'

'Oh no, I would sooner die than help you.'

My words may still have had the hint of fear, but it was

mostly venom that coursed through them.

'That is a shame. That would also be the incorrect answer that I previously mentioned.'

With that, I felt an invisible force shove me and send me flying backwards. My back hit a tree trunk with an impact that nearly winded me. She was in front of me then, hand wrapped around my throat and uttering some indecipherable incantation before I could even register her movement. I felt my powers bubbling beneath my skin as if they were being sucked to the surface. She was trying to take them, I realised. But I could feel them hanging on to me, trying to stay with me, burying deep into my veins, and the more she sucked, the more they glued to me. The vein in her forehead started to pulse and rise outwards. Her vicious eyes bored into mine, her grip around my throat tightening until I could hardly breathe at all. In the blink of an eye, a bright light burst out of my palms, and Titania got knocked onto her backside just away from me.

'HOW?!'

Her voice bellowed as she jumped to her feet. She was manic and raging now. I couldn't answer. Shock, fear, and confusion overwhelmed me. My powers had chosen me. I wasn't sure how I knew, but I had felt them rejecting her. There was a rage I had never seen before on her face. Clearly, she wasn't one to handle rejection well.

'You may have found a sneaky little trick to keep my powers from me, but they will do you no good here. I could just kill you, but I would rather know that you suffered.'

The absolute bitterness in her voice was glaringly obvious.

'You might feel like you have won, but do not be mistaken daughter. There are other ways for me to rebuild my powers and your little friends will be next to die.'

With that, she opened a portal and disappeared. I remained frozen in place by fear as my eyes scanned my gloomy surroundings. The dead forest.

Walking aimlessly in pure hope of finding an exit had seemed like a good idea until I was actually doing it. No trails or openings appeared, no matter how far I walked. Branches clawed at my skin as I tried to navigate my way through. One managed to scratch down my cheek, causing a light oozing of blood. Thistles scratched and grabbed at my torn trousers, trying to pull me down into the depths of the undergrowth. A deep thrumming ached in the back of my mind, and behind my eyes as my familiar bond cried at its separation from Saffie. I was determined not to cry, crying was not going to help. Even though all I wanted to do was to curl up into a ball on the floor and sob my heart out. I pushed the Prince, Saffie, and Aoife from my mind, thoughts of them were too distressing and I needed a clear head.

I had no idea how many hours I had walked for, but with aching legs and stinging wounds, I decided to take a break. Finding a patch that didn't have any spiky or nasty-looking vegetation, I slumped to the ground. Glancing down at my ogre fight wounds I noticed that they had been joined by a multitude of smaller ones, gained from my pointless wading through the forest. I didn't bother to check the rest of my body, I could feel that there were many more and to see them seemed pointless at this stage. I dropped my head back and closed my eyes, taking a minute to take some deep breaths in the hope that some genius plan would suddenly come to me. It didn't. Sighing in realisation that I had no idea how to survive or escape this woodland prison, I got back onto my feet. A sudden rustle from behind me woke my senses up very quickly. My instincts were screaming. I couldn't see it, but something was moving in the bushes. It circled around me, hidden. I felt for my weapon. Damn. I had no weapon anymore. I quickly searched the floor and lunged to grab a big stick. Before my fingers touched it, I felt a hard thud of something shoving me to the side. I landed awkwardly on the floor, but sprang back onto my feet, adrenaline surging. The thing was no longer hiding. It closed the gap too quickly. I couldn't stop my scream from piercing the silence. The creature stood just taller than me. A charcoal, scaly skin coated its body. Large, clawed hands and feet that looked ready to shred me glistened. But it was the huge predatory eyes, and piranha-like teeth that really made my blood run cold. The creature slashed its claws downward and tore across my chest and down my left arm. Without even needing to look I could tell that it had gotten me bad, as the wet warmth of blood soaked through my clothing and dripped down my body. Clinging my left arm close to my body and trying to hold my flesh together without looking, I ducked and rolled to avoid the next blow. Suddenly my body began to stiffen and a burning sensation radiated from my wound and spread to every inch of me. I couldn't move. Oh god, I was paralysed. I was paralysed, with a monster keen to eat me. If the beast could smile, I'm sure that was what it was doing as more of its horrifying teeth appeared visible. It stalked towards me, thick stringy saliva stretching nearly to the ground. All I could hope at this point was that these creatures were not ones to play with their food. If it went for my head first, then at least I would be dead before I felt it eat the rest of me. My thoughts briefly flickered over the Prince and Saffie. Would they ever be able to find out what happened to me? Would this creature leave behind any trace of me for them to find? Looking at its ravenous and emaciated appearance I could only assume it had no intention of letting any part of me go to waste. I closed my eyes as it stood over me and dropped its head down, mouth opening wide. I waited.

My breath held in expectation of death. But nothing happened. Then, a loud thud made my eyes snap open again. There was nothing above me anymore. I strained my eyes to the side and just about managed to see the lower half of the beast lying on the floor. It wasn't moving. Was this good or bad? Footsteps started sounding towards me. I darted my eyes around frantically, desperately hoping to see any one of my friends stride out from the bushes. But, the sense of danger that prickled my skin was making me aware that it was not them. Finally, a face appeared above me. He was Fae, that was evident from the pointed ears, and stern look on his face. Dark, thick stubble framed his lower jaw and top lip, and an unkempt mop of hair covered his head, some stuck down with sweat and other parts with foliage sticking out from it. His thick brow knotted together as he assessed me.

'You're human? I wasted my efforts on a human.'

His gruff voice held a note of surprise and disgust. He shook his head, appearing frustrated.

'Get up girl.'

I tried desperately to speak, to lift my hand, anything. But nothing responded. My eyes rapidly scanned the surroundings as he silently watched me.

'I said get up!'

His voice grew angry, and when I once again didn't respond he grabbed my arm and attempted to pull me up. As soon as he tried to pull, and realised my body was rigid, his brow knotted even tighter and he released me. My body thumped back down onto the floor.

'That toxin should only affect Fae.'

I could practically see the cogs turning in his head, but what conclusion he came to I couldn't tell as he walked out of my eyeline. I wanted to scream at him not to leave me, but also was grateful he had left me unharmed. I closed my eyes, the only part I had any control over. The Fae male's voice spoke from the back left of me. He hadn't left me. Although whether that would prove to be a good thing was yet to be seen.

'We need to wait a bit for the toxin to finish up with you. I reckon a couple more minutes and it should be over with.'

I desperately wanted to ask what he meant. Did he mean I would be free from the paralysis or that I would be dead? He surely wouldn't wait around though if he meant I was going to die would he? Unless... would he want to eat my body? I had seen a film about that sort of occurrence once, where people stranded on an island had killed and eaten each other to survive. Oh please God, I didn't want to become a victim of cannibalism.

It had to be the most awful few minutes, waiting to see if I would just suddenly start dying or not. However, as a pleasant surprise, I finally started to get a warm feeling start initially in my fingertips, and slowly spread through the rest of me. It took me a further couple of minutes to actually be able to move again, but when I could I nearly passed out as my new injury from the monster regained feeling. Eventually, I managed to roll onto my less attacked side and push myself onto my unsteady feet.

'Thanks.'

I managed to say, my voice not quite sounding normal.

'You look human, why?'

He stepped towards me, a sword shimmering in his

hand and a very mistrusting look on his face. So, definitely not out of danger yet then.

'I am human, sort of. I am half human, and half Fae.'

It still felt odd to admit that I was anything other than plain old human. I decided to leave out the part about Titania, who knew what would come of that revelation with this stranger.

'A half-breed? What realm are you from?'

The man's eyebrows shot up. I was really starting to detest that term.

'That is a long story. But, Unseelie... I guess.'

This was clearly the wrong answer as his eyes narrowed and his lips pursed in disgust.

'I am Seelie.'

His voice was curt, but his eyes were assessing me constantly. I remembered Aoife had once told me about the Seelie realm, and how it was like the enemy of the Unseelie realm once upon a time. She had told me about a treaty that had been formed to enforce a sort of peace between the two realms. She had made clear that there was still a lot of bad blood, but that they stayed out of each other's realms and business to avoid fracturing the agreement. Dealings were only done among the leaders of the realms.

'So, still want to stab me then?'

I nodded my head at the sword in his hand, a nervous chuckle escaping my lips. He glanced down at it briefly, as if he had momentarily forgotten he was holding it. He resheathed it in his waist belt before giving me a reluctant nod, and I managed to release the breath that I had been holding.

'I suppose in the dead forest, a half-breed Unseelie is better than no backup. I am Blake, Chief of the Seelie royal guards.'

CHAPTER TWENTY

RUBY

'So, Blake, fancy telling me where the hell we are going?'

My legs were still tingling but at least mobile now. I followed on behind him, my body tense and alert, ready for danger. I had categorically decided to ignore the slight spinning in my head, presumably from the extensive blood loss, and the searing pain all over my body. Now was not a time that I could afford to show weakness. He had helped me to rip a section of my trouser leg to tie a makeshift pressure bandage around the wound on my arm.

'Back to my... camp.'

He clearly couldn't bring himself to refer to anything in this place as home. Understandably. I wondered how long he could have been here for, and how a Fae of his high-ranking position could end up in this awful place. My lips twitched to ask the burning questions, but his no-nonsense and closed-off attitude suggested he was not up for a conversation.

Eventually, we reached a large rocked area, Blake

paused in front of it for a few seconds scouring his eyes over the surroundings. It was obvious that he was checking for dangers through his suspicious glances, before he finally pulled at the shrubbery covering the rock face. Flinging it to the side, he turned back towards me and revealed a cave entrance.

'You've got to be joking.'

The words tumbled out of my mouth without a thought, as I stared at the small dark entrance.

'You're welcome to stay out here and die if you would prefer princess.'

His frown and unimpressed tone suggested a slight bit of offense. The derogatory use of 'princess' that he had thrown my way was also a big clue that I had offended him. Now was not the time to piss off the only semi-friendly creature in this horrid place.

'I'm sorry... I was just a bit surprised.'

'You're surprised that there isn't some fancy castle that I've managed to acquire here? Well, I'm sorry that this cave is not up to your standards, but it's kept me alive since I got here so it's about the best damn thing you are going to get in this place.'

His typical Fae hardness slipped from his face ever so slightly. It was just for a second, but enough for me to notice the sadness there. He had said that he was from the Seelie castle, which meant that this was a far cry from what he was accustomed to also. I had no idea what to say, especially now that the infamous Fae wall of stone expression had returned to his face. So I nodded, and followed him into the creepy cave, begging the universe for him not to be a murderer or cannibal. How he could see what he was doing was beyond me, and after briefly bumping into him and mumbling an apology I glued myself to the nearest wall. I could hear him moving around, and then some loud banging noises before a spark of light flickered to life. It went out quickly, but he kept going until finally, he had created a flame that grew to life in a makeshift fire pit. The fire illuminated a large portion of the cave, and I felt my eyes grow wide as I took in how large it actually was inside.

'Bit more impressive than you thought? Sit down, unless you plan to stand until you drop?'

His lighter tone took me by surprise as he sat himself down on the floor and watched me curiously.

I gave a wary smile before sitting down with my back pressed against the wall. Whilst he seemed about as normal as a Fae could be, he was also a complete stranger in a place that was made to encourage killing. There was no way I was going to trust him.

'If I had wanted to kill you, I would have done it by now princess.'

I rolled my eyes, fed up already with this new insult, as if I hadn't had enough lately.

'I said sorry, no need for the princess dig to continue. How long have you been stuck here?'

I decided to brave the question, now that he looked as relaxed as he could probably be. His gaze dropped from me and he looked into the flame. His brow furrowed together in thought.

'It's hard to say, sunrise and sunset is skewed here. A couple of months I would guess though.'

My mouth must have dropped open because he looked back up and smirked.

'I know, it's amazing I'm still this devilishly handsome after being here for that long.'

Wow, this Fae had a sense of humour?

'Are you sure you're Fae? You seem too friendly to be.'

'This coming from the half-breed?'

I expected a hint of malice, but his expression was pure jest. This was not going the way that I had expected.

'I have spent two months on my own. I've been fighting for survival in this hell hole, and I have had no need to guard myself emotionally, just physically. If you had met me before I came here, you would have seen what you were expecting... probably worse. But now... well let's just say I am not ashamed to show that I am grateful to not be alone anymore.'

'I can understand why.'

I nodded, gazing towards the cave entrance, my mind imagining what could be lurking outside.

'So if you have been here that long, I assume that I can forget about a way to get out?'

My voice sounded closer to tears than I expected it to. I felt like I wanted to cry, but my body was struggling to fight the overwhelming exhaustion from the day.

'Not one that doesn't require magic, and we are fresh out of that in this place.'

My eyes snapped up as he said this. If there was no magic then how had Titania tried to siphon my magic and then created herself a portal? And how had my magic reacted against her? Come to think of it, I hadn't even noticed my magic's absence. But now, trying to dig into it, I realised it was completely dormant. I tried to think back to where I lost the feeling of it. The only thing I was sure of was that I had it when in the clearing in the woods.

'Well, there is actually one place that is a sort of clearing in the woods, a space where the magic barrier is thinner, and those that have enough power will be able to conjure magic there. I found it once before but my magic wasn't strong enough to conjure a portal with the barrier battling against it.'

'I've been there! It's where I came into this place!'

I tried not to mentally scold myself for just wandering from the one area that could have meant my escape. I knew my magic worked there, I had felt it. The question now was how much I could trust Blake. With my magic and Blake's knowledge, we might just be able to pull it off.

'So, you know how to get back there? And if we somehow had the magic needed to summon a portal then we can get out of here?'

'Maybe, but considering I have never heard of anyone escaping, I can't imagine how much power would be needed. I tried, many times, and I could barely even feel my magic, let alone release any. Do you have any magic in you? If so, perhaps between the two of us we can try and use our magic to even just send a message for help.'

I could see a serious thought process going on behind those eyes, but there was still mostly doubt. I wanted to tell him about my powers and give him a sense of hope, but I couldn't take that risk. He was still a stranger after all. I decided to admit that I had some power, so that he would remain hopeful.

'So that is settled then, we will help each other and get out of this awful place. You can go back to your Seelie realm, and me to the Unseelie realm.'

'Okay, but we should get some rest first. You don't look like you will make it five minutes out there currently.'

He definitely was not wrong. The adrenaline had completely left my body, and my eyes were becoming nearly impossible to keep open. Part of me knew that it could be dangerous to fall asleep, in this place and with this stranger, but my body was running on empty and couldn't function any longer. My eyes flickered closed and I relaxed into the darkness, just praying not to be eaten in my sleep.

ASH

Gone. She was just gone. The look of fear in her eyes, and Titania's cruel smile clawed angrily in my brain. If I had been here just a couple of minutes sooner I would have been able to stop this. A loud roaring cry from behind me averted my attention from the empty space of the closed portal. I turned to see Ruby's familiar staring straight ahead and trying to claw herself up off the floor. Her body did not respond enough though, and she slumped back down with a heavy thud. Her eyes closed as she lost consciousness again. A voice coughed from the side of me.

'Prince, a little help please?'

My friend had a greying complexion that indicated a concerning amount of blood loss. Unable to form any words, I silently moved towards her. I removed the knife in her right shoulder first, and she grit her teeth releasing only a hard hiss. The removal of the left-hand side knife however seemed to create a heavier blood flow and she cried out in pain. She fell to the floor, barely able to move. Instinctively I picked her up into my arms and carried her over to where Saffie lay unmoving.

'Saffie, you need to wake up. I can't get you back to the castle like this.'

My voice came out hard. I followed it up with a nudge from my foot, hoping to rouse her but not hurt her any further. With a groan her eyes flickered open, a pained expression painting her face.

'I need you to turn back, I can't get you back in this form.'

She whined before uncomfortably shifting back into her cat form. Her body, so small and fragile, looked broken. Kneeling, and balancing Aoife in one arm and over my knee, I used my other arm to scoop Saffie up and on top of Aoife. I formed a portal and carried them both through it.

Leaving them with Samira, I found Bran immediately and informed him of his wife's condition. His face drained of colour instantly and he sprinted to find her. Something inside me was telling me that Ruby was alive and I held on to that feeling in order to keep sane. Wherever Titania had taken her, she would be hidden well. There was only one person that I could imagine might be able to help. Refusing to acknowledge the growing feeling of loss, I stormed to find Delilah. I found her exactly where I had left her, but now standing over Katherine Sparrow's dead body. Her brow furrowed as she spotted me. A couple of her coven had been laid neatly on the floor, more dignified than the position they had died in.

'This is not the outcome we had agreed upon.'

'Titania took Ruby. I need you to do a locating spell to find her.'

She recoiled slightly at the tone of my voice, her face briefly showing a flicker of fear. I couldn't have cared if I tried though, my sole focus was to find Ruby.

'Forgive me Prince, but we have matters of our own to deal with. My sisters require urgent attention, and the matter of Katherine Sparrow needs to be dealt with. Justice must be served still. The families of the fallen witches must bear witness to her demise and she must be cursed in the afterlife.'

She answered nervously, gesturing around at her fellow witches who looked worse for wear.

'I do not care about any of that, you will perform a locating spell for me.'

She opened her mouth to protest.

'Now!'

I growled, striking complete fear and submission into her. I would need to mend that relationship at a later date, but for now, Delilah and her coven were nothing more than collateral.

I followed her to the table, where I stood on the opposite side of her.

'I will need something of Ruby's in order to try and locate her.'

Despite her fear, she had pulled herself together enough to stand tall and look frustrated with me. Running to her room to find items would take too long, so instead I held my hand out to her

'Use me. She and I are linked now, so that should work.'

The surprise on her face was not even remotely well hidden, but she did not utter a word about it. She pulled a tiny dagger from her cloak and took my hand in hers. I watched the blade slice from one side of my palm to the other, but felt nothing. My soul felt cold and dead, as though it had been ripped apart from me. Delilah began mumbling an indecipherable incantation, and the blood on the table began running in multiple directions. Her brow knitted together, and she began chanting more forcefully. The blood seemed to return her increased aggression and turned to some sort of acidic consistency as it burned its way through the table. She sucked in a breath, alarmed by the looks of it.

'She isn't anywhere.'

'What do you mean?' My voice came out threatening, and her discomfort was evident.

'Prince, I can not find her. That was a strong, and very precise spell, one that I've never had fight me like that before. I don't know how, but even magic can't sense her.'

I could see the look in her eyes, the one that held a mixture of sympathy and fear of saying the obvious; that Ruby was dead. But she wasn't. Every part of me could sense that her light had not been extinguished from this world.

'If you can not find her then I will find someone more competent.'

Normally this sort of insult would ignite a fiery response from Delilah, but in this moment she had the good sense to keep quiet and bow her head. Turning on my heel I exited the room.

CHAPTER TWENTY-ONE

RUBY

I awoke with an overwhelming disappointment as I realised that I hadn't been dreaming. I was indeed in a cave within the dead forest. I sighed and gripped my sore neck from an uncomfortable sleep on the hard floor. I glanced over and saw Blake asleep. Well, at least he hadn't killed me in my sleep. As I pulled myself up into a seated position, Blake's eyes popped open and he looked ready for action. I would guess that would be most people's abilities if they had resided in the dead forest for months.

'Morning princess.'

He groaned as he stretched out like a bear.

'Ruby.'

I corrected through an unladylike yawn. I heard him chuckle under his breath as he got up onto his feet.

'Ready to go?'

My stomach grumbled in protest, and I felt a warm embarrassed blush colour my cheeks.

'I'm guessing there's no food?'

'Depends whether you're hungry enough to eat what's available?'

He raised an eyebrow. I wasn't sure what that meant, but I knew I was not hungry enough to find out. I shook my head and dragged my sore and beaten body to standing.

'So, let's go then.'

I headed for the cave entrance, forcing myself to appear more energetic than I felt.

'Woah, woah there!'

He grabbed my shoulder and yanked me back. My heart jumped and my fist clenched ready to lash out in response to the agonising shooting pain down my arm. I span around, and he took a step back raising his hands in an innocent gesture.

'Just trying to stop you being shredded as soon as you step out. There's a whole host of beasts out there, you can't just go strolling out.'

Suddenly I felt completely idiotic.

'Oh... erm yes... that makes sense.'

I stumbled over my words, trying not to look like the most naive and clueless Fae possible. Pulling his sword, he rolled his shoulders back and moved cautiously towards the entrance. He pushed the foliage covering it to the side and waited before edging out. Then, As soon as he gave the signal I sprinted forward to follow him out. My heart pounded at the prospect of getting out of here.

Blake strode on ahead with ease through the forest, and I stumbled along behind trying to keep up.

'There's a river over this way, the water is drinkable from there.'

Blake glanced back at me and led me off to the right of the path we had been forging. My gasping and dry coughing must have signalled to him my need for water. He hurried me along and then returned us to our original track hastily. We managed a couple of hours before Blake stopped dead and forced an arm out at me to halt me in my tracks.

'You hear that?'

His voice was a whisper, eyes darting around like a rabbit sensing a predator nearby. I strained my ears but heard nothing.

'No.'

I whispered back. But as soon as I said it my hearing tuned into a quiet hissing noise. I couldn't focus on where it was coming from though, it seemed to be coming from every direction I turned.

'Snares.'

The word came through gritted teeth as he drew his sword. I didn't have to wonder for long what on earth Snares were, because one shot out at us, a loud hissing erupting from its mouth. It snapped at the air around Blake, trying to find an opening that wasn't guarded by his sword, its giant snake-like form moving ridiculously fast. I stepped back as Blake swung his sword with ferocity at the snare, not managing to land a blow, but successfully dodging the dripping fangs that lunged repeatedly at him. My skin crawled as a hiss came from behind me. By a stroke of luck, I managed to duck and roll away from the attack from behind. But it was quick to lunge again, and this time I had nowhere to roll. Instinctively I grabbed a broken branch nearby and smacked it around the head. It retreated for all of a second before coming at me again. This time though it grabbed my branch in its teeth, crunched it, and flung the pieces to the side. The fangs dripped as it edged closer, a predatory look of hunger freezing me in place.

'Ruby!'

Blake's voice shouted, and less than a second later a

dagger landed by my side. I grabbed the knife and as it struck once more I plunged the knife straight into the side of its hideous head. The creature screamed a horrifying noise, as it darted backwards and curled up. A yell made me turn quickly, in time to see Blake on the floor dragging himself backward and clutching his side. His beast pursuing him with the same predatory advancement that mine had. Without a thought, I threw myself up from the ground, lunged for Blake's sword, and took a swing at the giant snake. This one seemed more experienced than the one I'd faced. It bobbed and weaved every attack I made, and I soon realised it was wearing me out. This predator knew how to hunt effectively.

'Ruby, just run! Let it take me, and you can make it back to the cave.'

I didn't dare turn away from the beast, but it watched me carefully as if it understood the proposition. Its eyes assessed me, wondering what choice I would make. I could go, if I left Blake as a sacrifice. Hell no. As if sensing my resolve the creature narrowed its eyes, let out a gentle hiss, and struck speedily to my right-hand side. Its teeth snagged my clothing but thankfully missed my flesh as I jumped backward. This thing was working with brains, not just power. I hadn't a lot of space to work with, as I knew it'd take Blake and escape if I left him undefended for even a second. I swung some more, but it seemed to predict my moves and was dodging before I'd even committed to the move. It had been analysing me, learning my attack method, not just tiring me out. I had to change things up if I wanted to stand a chance of landing a surprise hit. In a moment of pure instinct, I swung my sword, knowing it would dodge, and instead of swinging again I darted backward picking up a rock as I went. I threw the rock, which bounded straight off its head, and provided the momentary distraction I needed to run and bury Blake's sword through its chest. The beast blinked at me for a moment, and I panicked it had been ineffective, but then it dropped down soundlessly.

'Why didn't you just run?'

Blake groaned as I knelt next to him, trying to gauge his injury.

'Because now we are even.'

I smiled, hoping my face wasn't showing the horror I felt at seeing the amount of blood oozing out of his side.

'It's okay, I know it's bad.'

His gritted teeth showed the agony he was feeling. I peeled his hands away and started to pull at the torn shirt sticking to him. Blood oozed from four holes that the Snares fangs had created.

'It's not the blood loss that will get me. It's the poison.'

'Oh sure, snakes have venom, that makes sense. It did look like a big, monster version of a snake.'

I was blabbing mindlessly as I tried to wrack my brain for any form of medical knowledge. Pressure. I needed to stop the bleeding with pressure.

'We need to get your shirt off.'

'I don't think now is the time for that, but if you insist on making my dying moments happy..."

He laughed a little too hard and started coughing horribly. Clearly the poison was having an effect.

'I need it to make a pressure bandage.'

I clarified, hoping my serious tone would encourage him to retain his wits. He grabbed my hand, a moment of sense washing over his face.

'I'm not going to be able to get back to the cave, and you will not survive out here for long. More creatures will come when they smell my blood. You need to go.'

'Not a chance.'

'Ruby, this is not up for debate.'

'You're damn right it's not, I am getting us both out of here. Now you can either help me or if not then just lay there quietly whilst I think.'

He seemed to think for a minute, assessing me, before his face scrunched and he let out a deep groan of agony.

'Okay, but I need this poison out or else I don't stand a chance regardless of your pressure bandage plan.'

His voice was becoming weaker. I helped to remove his top and then used it as a pressure bandage around his waist. Purple had spread like spider webs out from each bite wound. Poison. How the hell does someone remove poison? My instant thought was sucking it out, but I quickly tossed aside that gross and highly ridiculous idea. But what other option was there? I needed to get him to someone with knowledge of this sort of thing, someone like Samira. For that though I needed to find a way back to the clearing in the woods. I glanced around at my surroundings, still no clue where we were or where we needed to go.

'How far is it to the place where magic can be used?'

I shook Blake slightly until he reopened his eyes and squinted off into the distance.

'We are actually really close. But I won't make it, maybe just leave me here.'

He released a bear-like yawn.

'Pull yourself together, I need you to direct me. Can you stand if I help you?'

I asked, he nodded, so I put his arm over my shoulder and my arm around his waist and proceeded to help heave him up off the floor. He barely made a sound but I could tell it was excruciating for him.

'Well, who would have thought I would come to the

dead forest and have a princess put her hands around my waist.'

He chuckled giddily to himself. I could only pray for a miracle that he stayed lucid enough to direct me to where we needed to go.

'So, how about we go over this portal creation business?'

I urged him to talk me through the process over and over partly so that I could confidently do it, and partly to keep him conscious.

Blake's need for support increased the farther we walked, as he became weaker physically and dipped in and out of deliriousness. My breathing was becoming unbearably heavy, my already sore body struggling to fight through the pain, and my brain in complete overdrive trying to navigate through Blake's half-nonsense directions, whilst monitoring for enemies. Just as I felt like hope may have been lost, I sensed a feeling of warmth inside me. Magic. My magic was stirring as though starting to rouse from a deep sleep. We were close. Now ignoring Blake's rantings, I followed my senses until I finally dragged us to the place where I had first been dropped into the hell hole called the dead forest.

'We made it Blake! We bloody made it!'

I glanced to my side to see my companion was no longer talking and was barely holding onto consciousness. His weight was becoming too much. I hadn't ever made a portal successfully on my own before, but Aoife had told me about the process previously and Blake had repeated it to me up until he was no longer making sense. I also knew I had to make it work or we would definitely die soon. No pressure then. Summoning every ounce of my diluted magic I could grab hold of, I scrunched my eyes closed and thought of the castle medical suite as hard as I could. I thought of Samira, and her herbs, and bandages. Opening my eyes, I expected to have failed but was indescribably relieved to see a green portal glow in front of us.

'We are going home, you're going to be okay.'

I wheezed to Blake as I dragged his limp body through it.

'Oh my goodness! Ruby? What has happened?'

I heard Samira's sweet voice before my eyes adjusted and found her. She ran over and immediately began trying to examine me.

'I'm fine. Please help my friend, he was bitten by a Snare, he's been poisoned.'

Her alarm grew as she took in Blake's greying complexion. She immediately swung his arm over her shoulder and helped me drag him to a bed. She was surprisingly strong for someone so petite.

Ruby?

As soon as I heard my familiar's voice in my head, my heart felt like a missing piece had been restored. I instantly spun and found her tiny feline form on a bed nearby.

'Oh, Saff! Thank goodness you're okay!'

I ran and grabbed her into my arms.

Don't squeeze me, idiot, I'm injured!

I put her down quickly.

I was worried sick about you Ruby, what happened?

'I promise I will explain later, but I need to check on the others and let them know I'm back and tell them about Titania.'

Aoife was released to go home with Bran earlier, I have no idea where the Prince is though. Go, I will be here for another day or so apparently so I won't be going anywhere. I heal fast, but broken ribs take a bit of time.

I placed a kiss on my best friend's head.

'Samira, please let me know as soon as Blake is awake again.'

She nodded her head before continuing to spread some disgusting sludge over Blake's wounds. Saying goodbye to Saffie I hurried off to find Ash.

'Ruby?'

A voice called out as I made my way down one of the hallways. I turned to see Delilah's panic-stricken face. Before I could even ask, she wrapped her arms around me.

'Thank the magic you're alive. Where have you been?!'

I couldn't hide my shock as I pulled away and gaped at her. We were not friends, so why would she care if I was alive?

'It's a long story, had a quick stop off at the dead forest, but I'm back now.'

I tried to peer around her, looking for anyone else.

'The dead forest? Of course! That is why I couldn't locate you, the magic barrier would have prevented it.'

'I'm sorry Delilah, I really must go.'

I tried to step around her but she matched my steps and remained in front of me.

'The Prince has been going mad with worry, I have never seen him like it. The anger was actually frightening.'

My brain was struggling to take in what she was saying as my exhaustion was overwhelming, but Delilah actually looked almost tearful which roused my attention.

'Where is he?'

My pulse quickened and she gulped nervously.

'Delilah! Where is he?'

My voice raised as a nauseating feeling crept inside me.

'He said he was going to find someone else to help him when I couldn't locate you. But I've been tracking him because I was worried, he seemed like he had gone mad.'

She paused, as if expecting me to have a go at her, but I simply nodded to encourage her to continue 'He went to see a friend of mine, and when I called her she hadn't been successful either with her location spell for you, but he asked her to do another one afterward...'

'Who for?'

'Titania.'

As soon as the name escaped her mouth, my head began to spin.

'I'm going to need you to tell me exactly where he is.'

My fingers gripped her arm in a warning, my voice sounding its own kind of mad. He wouldn't have gone alone, would he? He wasn't that dumb. The look on Delilah's face suggested otherwise though. If the Prince had gone to face my crazy mother, then I needed to find him before he got himself killed.

CHAPTER TWENTY-TWO

RUBY

Having my palm sliced and blood squeezed out of it was less painful than I had expected, though perhaps that was only because I was so tense and desperate that my body couldn't focus on any other feelings. I resisted the urge to scream at Delilah to hurry up as she mumbled some chant. At any other time I would have found it fascinating to watch my blood swirl and move across the floor into the shape of a small map. A bigger blob indicated where the Prince was. Though I had no idea where that was in the Fae realm. I glanced up at Delilah who was frowning and tilting her head, analysing it.

'Do you know where that is?'

I asked with a snappy tone that I hadn't intended to have.

'I think... I think so. It looks like an area right on the border of the Unseelie territory. You see that there, I think that is the old sacred willow tree'

She pointed her long, perfectly manicured finger at a spiky-looking blob of blood.

'Remind me to ask about that later, when we survive Titania.'

'We?'

Her face went sickly grey at the suggestion.

'I need directions, nothing more.'

I rolled my eyes, patience completely non-existent in me now. She held out the knife she had used to cut me, and I absentmindedly took it, then she put out her empty hand towards me.

'Take my hand and create a portal, I will use my power to influence its location so that you end up there.'

She nods her head down at the blood blob representing the Prince. I did as she said, without hesitation, there was no time to question anything at that point.

My portal illuminated the room, and with a deep inhale I stepped through, not bothering to glance back at Delilah who fearfully waited on the safe side. The portal spat me out outside an old rundown building, a massive elderly tree hung a protective layer of branches and leaves over the front of it.

'You must be the sacred willow tree.'

I mumbled under my breath at the tree, hoping Delilah had sent me to the right place. Though, it didn't look much like what I had imagined Titania to be hiding out in. I hadn't thought of much of a plan, but walking in through the front door seemed like my only option at this point. She was unlikely to be expecting me at least, considering she had left me to die in the dead forest. Walking up the porch, I reached the front door which looked like it was barely hanging on its hinges. I carefully and quietly turned the old rusted door knob and crept in.

I clamped my hand down over my mouth as I unintentionally released a gasp of shock. The inside was beautiful. It reminded me of how the castle had looked in my dream that Titania had constructed previously. She must have had it spelled to look derelict on the outside, to remove suspicion. Clever. I paused for a minute, deciding whether to go up the magnificent staircase, or down the dimly lit hallway. My gut instinct told me to take the hallway. I gripped the knife so hard that my knuckles had turned a sickly white colour. As I wandered down the hallway that seemed too long for the building, I noticed a shadow up ahead, leaning against the wall. I raised my knife and crept forward. It took me a moment to notice the sword protruding from its chest. It was as I got closer that I recognised the impaled Fae. I blinked back the shock as I took in the face of my former friend. Oakley's body hung limp, his face grey, and a pool of blood at his feet. The prince had done this, I could just tell. Pushing the scene to the back of my mind, I marched onwards, reminding myself that time was of the essence. Continuing to follow my instinct I stopped at a door, sucked in a breath, and entered.

'Oh my god!'

I cried out as my eyes set on the Prince's beaten body chained to the far wall. He was on his knees, eyes glaring at the floor, but as soon as he heard my voice his head whipped up.

'What is this? Some kind of trick?'

I ran over and fell to my knees in front of him.

'No, it's me.'

I whispered so quietly I wondered if he would hear me. But the immediate twinkle of emotion in his eyes confirmed he had heard me. He raised his shackled hands to cup my face. His eyes were bloodshot, the left one starting to swell underneath, and a large cut split his lower lip apart. My heart ached to see him in that condition.

'She, she told me you were dead.'

His voice was more raw than I had ever heard it.

'It will take more than a forest of monsters to finish me off.'

I chuckled, gripping his hands tightly to my face, relishing feeling his touch. The clanging of his shackles from his shuffling brought me back to reality.

'We need to get you out of here.'

'These are warded so that I can't use magic. I can't free myself.'

He stared down at his hands and feet. I held my hands out, palms facing his binds, closed my eyes, and let the warmth of my magic flow through my hands. The ping of release let me know it had worked.

'How did you learn to do that?'

The prince raised an eyebrow, a proud smirk forming on his lips.

'I honestly don't know how to explain it, but since my magic chose me, I can feel it and just seem to know how to use it.'

'What do you mean your magic chose you?'

I had forgotten that he had no idea what had happened in the dead forest.

'I'll fill you in later, let's just get out of here.'

I helped to pull him to his feet. As we began to walk towards the door, we both jumped backward as it flung open. Titania's face filled with shock as her eyes flitted between me and the Prince. Then, it turned to rage. With a scream, she flung her hands out and sent us both flying backwards. I jumped straight back onto my feet, the Prince however did not, but a quick glance back at him showed me he was breathing at least.

'You are supposed to be dead.'

Pure rage spilled out from Titania as she stomped forward, immense hatred seeping from every angle of her.

'spoiler alert, I'm tougher than you gave me credit for.'

'I will end you for good you worthless, pathetic little human.'

'Go on and try it you old hag.'

I was ready to end this. My so-called 'mother' was going to die for good this time. I felt the next blow before I saw it coming, but rather than flinging me backward it hit me from higher up and knocked me down onto one knee. The force was enough to nearly wind me, and my knee crunched under the weight as it hit the floor. My snare injuries were incapacitating me far more than I had considered. But, refusing to bow down to her, I picked myself up onto my feet in time to feel the next wave of power that pushed me from behind and sent me falling forwards. My head smashed into the floor. My vision span. A warm wet feeling trickled down the side of my face, presumably blood from the head injury. I hesitated before getting up, inwardly begging my magic to spark to life. As if it heard my silent cry, I felt that now familiar warmth spreading through me and I raised my hands to send my own attack. She slid backwards and caught herself from my small but effective blast. With ridiculous speed, she had raced towards me and her fist collided with my cheekbone. She followed it up with a punch to my stomach, making me curl over. Her fingers gripped the hair close to my scalp and smashed my face off of her knee. I was then tossed onto the floor, on my side.

'I have to say, surprise does not quite describe my

response to finding out that you and this imposter Prince are now connected.'

She strolled towards me. I wanted to run, but the agony kept me curled up in a foetal position.

'I couldn't work it out at first, how you could hold onto my powers against my will. Now, though, it makes sense. You are very cunning dear daughter. Using your own poor half-breed powers to contain mine within you. Very clever indeed. But, you chose the wrong side.'

She snarled, and followed up with a hard boot to my stomach. She began to lift her hands and the realisation hit me that I was about to die. By some stroke of luck, the Prince had regained consciousness and shouted from across the room, which provided enough distraction for me to give us a final shot.

As Titania's head turned briefly I pushed myself to stand, the heat under my skin increased to the point of nearly unbearable. Fighting through the spinning in my head and my wobbly vision I focused every last conscious effort onto my target. She released another wave of every-thing she had, but time seemed to slow for me. I erupted with every last drop of energy I had, my only hope of survival. My force hit hers and fought against it. I hung on, fighting against the urge to drop. Slowly, my light consumed hers until it reached her and a blood-curdling scream erupted. She hit the floor, writhing in pain before becoming still. Short, shallow breaths were the only sign of her clinging to life. I hesitated before deciding to go over. Her eyes were losing their spark, but she managed to capture my gaze.

'You will regret this. I was the only thing holding him back. I wanted to return the world to its former glory, he wants to destroy it.'

'Who? What are you on about?'

I grabbed her by the shoulders and frantically shook, scared she would leave me in the dark about this new unknown threat.

'I only wish now that I would be around to watch your brother burn you all to the ground.'

The words barely came out, but the venom was there until she drew her last breath and blood spilled from her lips. My brother. I had a brother. A brother, who according to Titania was a raging psychopath as well, potentially a pyromaniac if I were to take what she said literally. How could I have had a brother and not known? A scratching in my head made my eyes wince, as my mind desperately tried to capture the thought that seemed to be stuck out of reach. I glanced around the room, taking in the surroundings. Now looking at it, it was a replica of the room in the castle that my dream had taken place in. Staring me in the eyes from every angle I turned was Titania's portrait on the walls, and... damn it. The sudden realisation hit me like a huge thump to the skull. The man featured in some of her portraits. It was him. I'd had a feeling in my dream that I knew him, but I had never worked out who he was. I had forgotten about him, assuming he was some distant relative long gone. It seemed so obvious now as I assessed his features. His face shape, his eyes, the curve of his lips, they were the same as mine. Stunned, it took me a moment to register the Prince limping up to me in my peripherals. I turned to look at him, battered and bruised but somehow still managing to hold that strong look that made me feel safe. Without saying a word he created a portal, which to the untrained eye would have looked effortless. But I could see the ever so slight crinkle of his eyes and stiffened posture that revealed his pain. He reached for my hand, intertwining our fingers. A gesture so human I was momentarily lost in the thought of us in a normal human life together. But, the sickening feeling I got every time I went through a portal reminded me that it was just a thought, never to be a reality, and now my reality was about to become a whole lot more complicated. As I stepped through behind the Prince, a voice made me turn just in time to see him standing there over our mother's body.

'I never did see value in her plan. I will see you very soon, little sister.'

Those manic eyes bored straight into mine right up until I disappeared through the portal.

CHAPTER TWENTY-THREE

RUBY

Stepping out of the portal and into the safety of the castle allowed me to breathe an involuntary sigh of relief. We had made it. Every inch of me was screaming in agony, I was surprised at my ability to remain upright at this point. I looked up from my feet to see the faces of the king and a selection of the king's guards. An uncomfortable feeling turned my stomach. Their faces were not ones of delight at our return.

'Seize her.'

The King ordered. Immediately hands gripped me and pulled me from the Prince. His previously slumped form perked instantly and he began to shove the guards away until three of them managed to hold him back.

'What are you doing?!'

Weighted metal cuffs clicked shut over my wrists, and I felt my power slink back inside me, out of reach. These were the same as what Titania had used on the Prince, I recognised. My powers were no longer accessible, the warmth of their fire dying down inside me. Fury raged in the Prince's eyes, his voice raw with anger.

'What are you doing?! Unhand her!'

Even I flinched back, but despite the obvious discomfort of those detaining me, they held firm and looked to the king for confirmation.

'You forget your place son. I am king, they follow my orders. She is now a prisoner of the Palace.'

'Under what charges?'

'Conspiring against the King, and trying to assassinate the Prince.'

'What?! She has done no such thing! I am only alive as a result of her saving me. She has killed Titania, she has eradicated any threat. You should be thanking her!'

I had never heard the Prince so flustered and out of control. It felt wrong.

'Take her away, and detain the Prince in his room until further notice.'

The king waved his hand, dismissing us. I wanted to shout and scream, and fight back, but I had nothing to give. My body, after all it had endured, was fighting to keep me upright, and my brain was too tired and baffled to comprehend the situation. Dumbfounded, I allowed myself to be dragged down some cobbled stairs I hadn't known existed in the Palace. As we reached the bottom of the stairs and reached the end of a dark dank corridor, realisation hit me. I was a prisoner, and this was my prison. Of course one of the guards had to be Sophie. Undoubtedly she was enjoying this moment.

'Please don't do this.'

My voice came out as a pathetic squeak. For a second I thought Sophie seemed to show a flicker of guilt, but It was gone again so quickly I couldn't tell if I'd imagined it.

Neither guard answered me. Instead, they continued to drag me and eventually threw me into a rusty, iron-barred cage. They walked away and left me. The harsh rocky wall ensured a too cool temperature that I knew would leave me shivering soon. Glancing around my cage, I noticed my toilet was just a dirty-looking bucket. Rodent droppings littered the floor. There was no bed or blankets. It was clear this place was intended to deliver a slow, torturous death to its inhabitants. My brain whizzed over the events that had unfolded in the last 24 hours. I had escaped the dead forest, saved the Prince, and killed Titania. Yet here I sat in a prison cell for it. I had been warned about the King. Even Titania herself had warned me, but I'd been so caught up with the threat of her that I'd completely ignored the threat right under my nose. I stood, unwilling to move for a while, though I couldn't tell how long. Footsteps sounded down the corridor and I leaned forward, avoiding touching the bars, to try to see who was coming. Had the Prince been able to get me freed?

Eventually, they came into sight. The same two guards that had delivered me here. This time though they were holding something. Saffie. She was in her cat form and unmoving in one guard's arms. She was carelessly tossed into the cage next to mine.

'What have you done to her?!'

I ran to the side of my cage that was attached to hers. I stretched my arm through but couldn't reach her. Breathing, was she breathing? My own breath halted as I anxiously watched until she drew in a slow inhale and then exhaled. Breathing, but unconscious.

'It was a sedation, she should wake up in a couple of hours.'

A guard called back as they disappeared from sight. I

slunk down to the floor, no longer caring that I was not only touching the gross bars but my face was pressed against them too. I continued to sit, watching Saffie breathing, and replaying the scene of being imprisoned over and over in my mind. If my stress were not so high I was pretty sure I would have collapsed by now. If I hadn't been Fae I would have definitely been dead by now. But then, if I weren't Fae then I never would have been in this situation. The endless thoughts raced around my brain, only really serving to exhaust me even further.

Eventually, Saffie's breathing increased and her muscles started twitching as she regained consciousness.

'Saff, can you hear me?'

My voice came out hoarse as though I'd been crying, and I soon then realised I must have been as my cheeks were cold and wet, and damp pools of tears had soaked a patch on my top. She let out a weak growl

'I would say it's okay you're safe, but that would be a lie.'

I attempted a slight sense of humour to my tone.

Glad I can rely on you to keep the spirits lifted. If this is what we are now going to be living in, please call them back and ask them to sedate me again.

She grumbled as she looked around at our surroundings. Even with a dazed appearance, her horror was very much visible.

'Not quite our bedroom upstairs in the castle is it.'

So, not that I mind being thrown into disgusting prison cells, but what exactly did you do to land us in here?

She continued to glance around, pure disgust showing as her lip curled and her ears pinned back.

What the hell happened to you? You look like you have been hit by a bus.

She then remarked as her eyes finally settled on me and took in my appearance. I hadn't seen my reflection since I had returned, but I could imagine I was not a pretty sight to behold.

'Oh you know, save the Prince, kill Titania, classic evil plans. Apparently, all of that is tantamount to treason in the King's eyes.'

I rolled my eyes, trying not to let more tears fall out.

You killed Titania?!

Saffie sat bolt upright and stared at me, assessing me for some hint of joking. Apparently that was the most surprising part.

'Yes, and as it goes I have an evil brother too. Though I don't suppose that will matter if the King plans to kill us.'

I think you will need to start again, either you're skipping a lot of details, or the sedation has left my brain mashed.

Saffie's paw brushed over her eyes as though her head was aching. Taking a deep inhale, I did my best to relax a bit and let loose to Saffie all of the events that had happened.

Well, I did warn you about the King plotting something.

'Really? I told you so now?'

So, let me just clarify, the King now knows that you are Titania's daughter and wants you dead, and me dead by default too. You have found out that you have somehow mashed up your own half-breed powers with Titania's stashed ones and now are a bit over-powered. Titania is already dead , as you killed her, but she was actually the sane one in your family and now you have a psycho brother on the loose who wants to kill everyone?

'I would say that sums it up mostly yes.'

Couldn't just be a normal and boring half-breed Fae could you?

She chuckled, probably half serious though.

'So I see you've got the matching necklace to my bracelets.'

I pointed to the metal cuff around her neck that resembled the cuffs on my wrists.

No panther shifting for me. I guess my smaller claws are preferable to them

'Can't you squeeze through the bars?'

Without this contraption on my neck, sure, but not with it on.

ASH

Looking around my upturned bed chambers I finally sighed and slumped to the floor in exhaustion. Despite the definite broken ribs, searing pain radiating from the swelling around my eye, and every other bruise covering my body, my biggest pain was emotional. Ruby had been taken from me. Not just taken though, cuffed and escorted to a cell like a prisoner. The look on her face as they dragged her away was one that I was sure would haunt me forever. As soon as they had practically carried me to my room and secured the door, I had let loose an absolute rage. All pain had been replaced with anger and adrenaline. My room now had pieces of broken furniture scattered around it, and holes in the walls and en-suite door. She had rescued me, I'd been certain I was going to die when I lost my fight to Titania. But then Ruby came in and saved my life. She had a habit of doing that, even when she didn't realise she was doing it. I had awoken in time to see the sheer strength and power she possessed, it was like nothing I had ever seen before. Ruby had already got my heart and respect for who she was, but I felt complete admiration towards her in that moment, the most powerful Fae I had ever laid eyes upon. It had taken me longer than I would be proud to admit, but the mystery over her powers finally made sense to me. Delilah's comment about her 'two powers' had played on my mind ever since she had said it, but it was Titania's that put the pieces together. There was a small but noticeable difference in their magic, which wouldn't be possible if it were indeed solely Titania's powers. Now that I had realised it, I felt a fool. It was obvious. Ruby was a half-breed, and so had her own magic. Her magic, mixed with powers from one of the most powerful Fae in history had led to an excessively strong level of magic within her. Now though, to imagine her sitting there in one of those disgusting cells like a criminal, rather than being celebrated like the hero she was, made me feel absolutely sick to my stomach. What was my father's game though? I had known that our secret was lost the minute that Katherine had revealed Ruby to be Titania's daughter. I had felt his icy stare for the brief moment before I had launched at Katherine. This was more than that though, he had concocted a lie about her trying to kill me. The only possible cause that I could assume was that he had discovered our connection.

I sat for at least an hour pondering over conversations that I had been excluded from, wondering what plotting had been being done by my father. I deduced in the end that he must have created this plan to prevent rumours of a conspiracy against him. It would look terrible if his only son, Prince to the throne, had consorted with Titania's daughter by choice. But that still didn't explain his indication of longer imprisonment. I would have expected mention of execution within twenty-four hours, but there had been nothing said on that matter. I'd had no real fondness for my father before this, but I did have respect. Emotions were hard to conjure towards a parent who had never shown you any. But now, my respect was gone and my only emotion was a burning anger that was demanding revenge. All my father had ever cared about and wanted was power, he was determined to remain King at any cost. Suddenly it hit me, her power. He wanted her power and that was why she was still alive. My mind wandered back to a previous conversation that I had brushed off and forgotten about. How could I have been so stupid and careless? It was my fault Ruby was in that cell right now. I had been in the know the whole time, and had been too idiotic to see it. Well, now it was time to do some plotting of my own. She had managed to save me, and now it was time to return the favour. The first task was to figure out a way out of this room.

CHAPTER TWENTY-FOUR

ASH

As I peered downwards I could only be grateful that I had not been cursed with height phobias. My back remained tightly pressed against the harsh stone walls, my toes just peeking over the edge. My plan had seemed simple at the time; exit through the window, and shuffle along the windowsill ledge until I reached Aoife and Bran's room next to mine. It seemed more inconspicuous than incapacitating the guards holding me hostage.

Bursting in through Bran and Aoife's window was a strategy based on my needs. More specifically my need to save Ruby. However, I had not considered the needs of my friends at that time. In fact, I probably hadn't considered their personal needs for many years, if ever. It was this ignorance that led me to encountering quite possibly the most uncomfortable situation imaginable with my friends. I awkwardly averted my eyes as they scurried to pull the bed covers over themselves.

'Prince... how can we...'

Bran began, but was quickly interrupted by a less accepting Aoife.

'What in Fae hells are you doing bursting in like that?! And through our window of all things! Have you never heard of knocking on one's door?'

It was scary how much Aoife was beginning to sound like Ruby. I wanted to comment on the inappropriate tone that she had taken with me, but reconsidered based on the circumstances.

'I need your help. Surely you heard?'

'Heard what?'

Bran asked, cutting off what looked like was going to be a sarcastic retort from Aoife.

'Ruby. The King has sent her to the cells. She has been arrested for conspiring against the King and trying to kill me.'

'What?'

Aoife's voice took a shrill tone.

'He knows everything, and now he wants her powers. He will do anything to take it and possess it.'

'What are we going to do? We can't go against the King.'

Bran's voice sounded conflicted. It was a mental war that I understood all too well. The love for my father was not there and so that did not concern me, however the loyalty to my King was strong. We were all conditioned to be relentlessly loyal to the King, and the prospect of going against him troubled us deep to the core. However, as I was finding, there were things that rivalled and even ran deeper than loyalty to the throne. The mental image of Ruby sitting in a cell made my blood boil, and a nauseating feeling rolled over me continuously like a series of waves. I couldn't leave her there, nor could I allow my father to steal her powers and destroy her.

'I'm in. I will follow you into any battle Prince, my loyalty lies with you and Ruby.'

Aoife dipped her head briefly, indicating her allegiance. Bran observed his wife for a second before nodding his head back to me. I thanked them both for their loyalty to me and even to Ruby.

'What's the plan?'

Bran asked, voice now firm and secure in his decision.

'I'm going to challenge the king.'

I hadn't decided until that second. I had weighed up freeing Ruby and escaping, trying to reason with my father, and faking her death. However, the only option that secured her safety was to challenge my father for the throne. I knew he would never stop trying to claim her power, and she would be his prisoner until he finally managed it. I also knew that whilst he did not want to kill the heir to his throne, that option was not off of the table in his mind.

'Bran, I need your help to ready me. Aoife, I want you to find a way to Ruby and let her know I'm coming for her. I can only imagine how she must feel down there'.

They both agreed to help me, but seemed concerned still. I stood for a moment waiting for them to spring into action.

'Prince, I will follow you into any battle, but not naked. Please at the very least turn around for a moment.'

For a moment, all three of us began laughing and my mind raced back to memories of our younger years. To think, that could be the last time that I might reminisce with them.

RUBY

Ready to give up yet?

Saffie commented as she watched me stalking my cell like a caged beast. I had rattled every bar on it, hoping to find a slightly loose one. There were none. I then tried to find loose bricks in the wall. There were none. Despite the dilapidated appearance of the prison cells, they were damn sturdy.

'There has to be a way out!'

I growled, my anger driving me on.

This isn't some film Ruby. This is a Fae prison, they do not risk losing prisoners.

She sighed, clearly more resigned to our fate than I was. Or perhaps she was just not as naive as I was.

'Well we cant just sit here waiting to die Saff! Newsflash we are in enemy territory and we are losing!'

You're getting hysterical.

She was right, my voice had reached a squeaky frequency and my pulse was racing uncomfortably. But there was no way I was stopping or calming down. If I calmed down I would cry, and that was not something I was willing to do at this point. Sensing my desperation, Saffie rolled her eyes and began nudging the bars of her cage. I smiled gratefully at my friend as she repeated my steps in trying to find an escape possibility. Meanwhile, I continued to pace and examine everything over and over. I wondered momentarily if this was how caged tigers in the zoo felt as they paced back and forth eyeing the enclosure and the world outside their prison.

After a while, Saffie gave up trying to pacify me and sat herself down quietly. She watched me until I finally gave up and slumped down next to her.

The Prince will come for us.

Saffie attempted to console me, though she didn't sound convinced.

'Sure, if he manages to escape his own prison.'

It was hard to assume how much time passed before we heard more footsteps coming down, though it felt like hours. Saffie leapt to her feet and she assumed a defensive position, ready to attack.

Ready yourself, Ruby, someone is coming. We may need to fight our way out of here.

Her voice growled inside my head. My pulse quickened again as I scrambled up and took a deep breath. The footsteps grew louder, and the tension rolling off us both grew with it, until finally, a familiar face appeared.

'Aoife!'

My voice whined, threatening to break and release tears. Then I found myself quickly questioning her reasoning for being here. However, her expression of sympathy and disgust helped me to push those feelings down, and my hope began to grow again. I was getting out of here.

'Please tell me you're here to get us out?'

I sighed, a slight hysterical giggle leaking in to my tone. I expected a sassy smile, but my hope dropped again as her head gently shook, an apologetic smile touching her lips.

'I'm sorry, I can't. But I am here to let you know that the Prince is going to get you out soon, I promise.'

Her words were confident but nervous at the same time. A strange combination for someone who was providing what should have sounded like good news.

What's the catch?

Saffie beat me to the question. Aoife sucked in a breath uncomfortably before answering.

'To get you out, the Prince is having to take certain measures that will take a bit of time, but I am confident he will succeed.'

That was elusive. Too elusive. Something was definitely wrong.

'I am sure you can be a bit more specific than that Aoife.'

'The Prince has challenged the King.'

The words tumbled from her lips hastily. Saffie gasped out loud, which made me jump.

'Challenged him to what? What am I missing here guys?'

Fae rules meant that to override the King's decisions, the Prince must become the King.

I stared at Saffie, waiting for further clarification.

The prince needs to defeat the King in battle Ruby.

'What?! He needs to kill his own father?'

He doesn't have to kill him necessarily

'He doesn't have to, no. But it would be shameful for the King to live under the Prince's rule through battle defeat, the King will choose death and the Prince will not strip him of that dignity.'

Aoife added, too calmly.

'Surely there is another way?'

'No. The King had the option to decline the challenge and resign from his position, thus passing it down to his son. But the King did not wish to do that, he accepted the challenge.'

'And if the Prince does not win?'

'The King will not keep a son who challenges him alive.'

Aoife's voice shook for the first time since I'd met her. She was scared for him too. I hadn't seen the King fight, but surely he could not be as strong or fast as Ash?

'I have to go, I need to help the Prince with his preparations.'

She turned to leave, but then hesitated and turned back and walked up to the bars. She stood very close, and beckoned me towards her.

'The Prince will succeed Ruby, but if anything goes wrong then be ready for a plan B escape, I will get you both out.'

Aoife, you risk your life planning something like that.

'I have learned a lot since meeting you two, and you have irrevocably changed my life and my perception of the world. I love the Fae Kingdom, but I can't allow it to take the people I care about from me. You may have to just help me and Bran to adjust and hide in the human world though.'

Tears moistened my eyes, and I gripped her fingers around the bars in a comforting gesture. she laughed, sadness in her voice. With that, she turned and quickly walked away.

How are you feeling?

Saffie asked, clearly concerned

'Sick with worry. How about you?'

Same. We are about to either have a more intense life in the Unseelie realm, or we are about to make a risky run from it.

'And the Prince may not make it through to run with us.'

My voice shook. The Prince was challenging his own father to rescue me. He would have to kill or be killed by his father. Faerie Law was sick. It did occur to me that this world seemed to be very at ease with matricide and patricide. It was very concerning. I sat down at the bars next to

Saffie and held her paw through the bar, a gesture intended to comfort us both a little.

CHAPTER TWENTY-FIVE

ASH

'You are sure you are ready for this Prince?'

Bran asked as he helped me to dress for battle. To say my father had been surprised would be an understatement, the shock however had quickly turned to rage and disgust. His previously loyal son had turned against him. The look he had given me reminded me of being a young boy, and how I had been 'trained' to display undeniable loyalty to the King. At first, I had been resentful as a child, but the ongoing beatings for my insolence helped to kill off my anger, and ability to feel much towards my father. Even as an adult, I didn't feel anger towards him for any of the past, but now with his treatment of Ruby, I found a renewed and refreshed level of rage towards him. I knew without question that my father would kill me if he were to win, he would not allow the royal traitor to survive as that would risk him looking weak and he would fear being challenged again. Losing could not be an option. My death would be quick, but Ruby would be left behind in that cell to rot, and that was not something I could allow to happen.

I picked up my sword, and gripped it tight, admiring the shine. I had slain many monsters and traitors with this sword but had never even considered killing my King with it. I was confident with this weapon. It had been forged for me specifically, and I had trained extensively with it. If I were a human I may have considered it my 'lucky charm'. My mind drifted to my father's weapon of choice, it would be his personally made sword too. My father had been in to battle and fought many enemies and won, his strength and speed were not something I would underestimate. I had been knocked down harshly enough times during training sessions in my youth to know that he was going to be a chal-lenge. His determination to keep his throne would certainly make him even more dangerous.

'I am sure.'

I finally responded to Bran. He searched my eyes briefly for any sign of indecision but must have been assured with what he saw, as he nodded in acceptance.

'Your father was a great warrior in his day.'

'I am aware.'

I did not appreciate his stating the obvious.

'But his day is no more. You can beat him. It is time Prince for you to step up and take over. The King is over-confident and has not trained in a long time, defend in the first instance and then attack when he begins to wain.'

'I'm not sure it's a skill that you forget when that expe-rienced.'

'No, perhaps not. But it is something you lose speed and endurance with though.'

With that Bran patted me on the shoulder.

'I'll see you out there Prince.'

Then he left the room. I waited for the door to close and for me to be alone before I squeezed my eyes tightly shut and took a few slow deep breaths. I had not particularly felt nervous before, but this time I felt a nauseous wave in my stomach. I was not scared to die, but I was scared of what would happen to Ruby if I were not able to succeed in this. It was so strange to consider how much this one not-so-human girl had changed my entire being. It was as though she had awakened me and given me a whole new view of the world.

Stepping out into the battle arena, the sun seemed to be brighter and harsher than before. I was impressed with the aesthetic make-over that had been done to display the royal nature of the battle. Deep red banners with the royal crown printed on them hung from the corners. A throne had been erected to one edge surrounded with flowers from the royal garden. The throne would be where the champion would take their place after the battle. Would this be me? Rows and rows of seats surrounded the battle area, and everyone was filled. It was unsurprising really. Fae were traditional in their ways and this was going to be a mark in history for us all, be it through the rise of a new king, or the death of the Prince and King's future successor. The crowd remained silent at my arrival, and there were many hushed whispers. Bran and Aoife sat front row and centre, their eyes firmly on me with unspoken support.

My father entered from the other side and raised his hand and sword as the crowd cheered. His devilish grin spread as he lapped up the shouts of loyalty. I noticed that Bran and Aoife remained silent whilst everyone else vocalised their support for their King. Many were grateful to my family for taking the throne from Titania so long ago, and if I were to be fair to him my father had provided the kingdom and its inhabitants with a relief from Titania's previous tyranny. For most, he had been a good and honest King. Those who saw him that way would not see me in a positive light... until they had to. Others would be caught in an awkward battle of uncomfortable loyalty. I had acquired a generally positive reputation across the kingdom, and many people were fond of me, but they would be duty-bound to support their King.

My father's eyes burned into mine, anger radiating from them. We both stepped towards each other in unison, not breaking eye contact. Bran stepped forward, as second in command to the King's guard, to begin the challenge. Professional to the core, Bran maintained a completely impartial composure in his speech.

'Welcome Unseelie realm. As many of you are aware, the Unseelie Prince has challenged the Unseelie King for his throne, and today we bear witness to this. The traditional rules of combat will be in play today.'

With this, he turned towards us, and his back to the crowd and addressed us.

'Raise your weapons in respect.'

We both obliged. With that, he took a few steps away.

'Ready your weapons competitors! Begin!'

We both brought our weapons down and positioned ourselves. With that, Bran moved quickly back to his seat. My father immediately started circling, and I quickly moved to match his pace. He swung first, a light blow that I easily blocked. He then tried from the alternate direction. He was easing himself in and sizing me up. I recognised that look on his face, it was the same one I had seen throughout my youth. His pupils had dilated and a sadistic smile spread across his face as he circled me like a predator hunting its prey. He launched at me again, with more ferocity this time and I quickly raised my sword to defend. His face began to shade a very slight red, indicating his increased effort. Bran's words rang in my head, I needed to tire him out. He was strong though, that certainly hadn't diminished with time, and so I had to make sure that I could hold out long enough to tire him.

'Come on boy, don't tell me your little human has made you so weak.'

He laughed breathily as he took another swing at me. He was speaking of Ruby to distract me, that was obvious. The problem was that it worked. I didn't raise my sword in time so had to duck out of the way. His sword cut down my left arm. Warmth spread through my arm and I felt my blood immediately begin to drench my skin and clothing. Holding in my groan of pain, I pressed my lips tight, not wanting to give him that satisfaction. The next blows came in quick succession and I worked hard to avoid any further hits, knowing that any more would be the end for me. Ignoring the searing pain down my arm, and the black spots threatening to claim my vision due to blood loss, I continued to dodge and defend. My father continued attack, both physically and verbally, but I had tuned his voice out and focused myself purely on his movements. I was waiting for the right opportunity.

Just when I thought that there would be no waning of his efforts, and my own energy was depleting rapidly, I noticed a small hesitation before his next swing. It was then I noticed that he had become more reddened in the face, thick saliva lined the corners of his mouth, and his chest was heaving violently. This was my moment. Summoning every last piece of my determination, I blocked his hit and shoved back as hard as I could. He stumbled backward, only slightly, but enough for me to pounce. My heart was pounding so hard that it was all I could hear. This time it was my turn to deliver the blows. He managed to block the first couple, but his defence was feeble. My third blow had his wrist bending unnaturally, so much so that his grip loosened and his sword fell to the floor. He quickly bent to grab it, but before he could rise I already had my sword point pressed against his throat. This was it, I had beaten him.

My father looked up at me, a brief moment of confusion lighting his eyes, but this was quickly replaced with rage and disgust.

'You are a disgrace to the throne! You and that human whore of yours will be the death of this realm.'

His spit landed on my wounded arm, and I made a mental note to thoroughly clean it later. The man cursing me as my sword pressed against his jugular should have conjured up some emotions from me, I know he should have. But he didn't. I had assumed I would feel more if I made it to this position, but to my surprise, I felt very little. I may have known him to be my father my whole life, but he had not been a good father. I may have known him also to be my King, but this bitter and feral-looking man bowed before me no longer appeared as the fearsome King I had sworn to protect. He now looked like a crazed King, one who had come to the end of his reign. A sense of closure washed over me as I realised in a matter of moments I would no longer live in the shadow of a father that couldn't love anyone more than himself and power, nor would I be under the control of a power-hungry King.

'My King, what do you choose?'

I hadn't even noticed Bran appear to the side of me until his voice cut through my thoughts. His voice was calm and collected, so much so that one would not imagine he was asking someone if they would like to die. The King looked between us, clearly torn. To ask for mercy would mean being labelled a coward, and his name forever tarnished. However, the alternative was no longer living. I hadn't expected my father to even consider the options, but I suppose in such a situation it must be difficult to ask for death.

'I will see you in the underworld boy, and believe me you will not escape me then.'

He growled at me, decision made, before closing his eyes and lifting his head ready to receive his fate. Bran nodded to me to confirm the decision had been made. Lifting my sword, I decided to make it swift and as painless as I could, as my final serving to the King.

CHAPTER TWENTY-SIX

RUBY

Time seemed to be stretching on forever. I laid on my back, eyes closed, ignoring the pounding in my head, and the disgusting floor touching my skin. It was hard to guess how long I must have been awake, but I knew it was an unhealthy length of time. I also knew that if my wounds and injuries weren't tended to soon then there was a chance of me dying from some sort of infection. Saffie was silent but I could feel her watching me. My mind felt like it was splitting into multiple people as one part screamed every worrying outcome that could come from this situation, another was crying about the Prince being in serious danger, and the other was telling those two to shut up. Is it possible I was going insane so soon after being imprisoned? I supposed after everything that had happened there was a very good possibility indeed of insanity.

'Would I know? If he died, would I know? With the connection we have, I feel that I would, but I don't know.'

My eyes remained closed. It definitely sounded like I was losing it.

I don't know in all honesty, but I imagine you would. Our bond means we would know with each other, so I presume it would be similar.

Saffie's voice sounded solemn in my head. Was she expecting the worst outcome? I squeezed my eyes shut tighter, trying to focus my mind on Ash. Ash, I hadn't used his real name much since he first told me it. It was funny really, to have continued calling him by his title rather than his name. The name felt strange when I linked it with his image, but I liked it. Surely my powers could help me, these cuffs couldn't be completely magic proof right? I tried for a good few minutes to conjure some sort of vision or feeling, before sighing in frustration and giving up. Distant footsteps had me instantly sitting bolt upright, eyes so wide they felt like they would pop from their sockets. Saffie responded as quickly, and we both stared ahead awaiting who was coming down the hall.

As Aoife's face came into view I made a noise that could only be described as an inhuman shriek or wail. My chest tightened and tears poured from my eyes as I failed to suck in air. Falling forward my hands splayed out on the ground in front of me. He was dead. If Aoife was here, it was because he was dead. My stunningly beautiful, secretly kind, and incredibly strong Ash was gone. Suddenly the cell door was flung open and hands were on me, shaking me violently.

'Ruby! Cut it out! He is fine, he won!'

Aoife's voice sliced through my absolute meltdown.

'What? He's alive?'

'Yes he is alive, I assure you.'

She was squatting in front of me, grasping my shoulders. Tears continued to pour down as I searched her face for any sign of a lie. She was smiling, but worried. It was the truth, he survived. Suddenly I could breathe again, and I inhaled so deeply I choked on it. I needed to see him, my heart was aching in a way I had never experienced before.

'Why didn't he come for me?'

I sounded pathetic but not a single part of me cared at this point. Why hadn't he been the first one down here to release me from this place?

'There is a lot that needs to be done, and quite a lot of smoothing things over was needed. He asked me to come and get you both out. But, he did it Ruby, he actually did it!'

Relief, happiness, and a touch of excitement all oozed from Aoife.

'I thought for a moment hope was lost, but the prince... Sorry the King, battled through and won.'

Her smile broke into a full grin as she changed his title.

'And his father?'

I almost dreaded asking, but I needed to know.

'Dead.'

She said it so matter of fact that it was easy to see how very Fae she still was at her core. How would Ash be feeling after killing his own father? He didn't seem to hold too much affection towards the tyrant, but it was his father after all. He had no parents at all now. Losing a parent is one thing, but killing them... Does that make him a murderer? I suppose only by human laws, but still dodgy ground right? Then again, that would make me as bad as I had just killed my own mother.

Aoife released us from our cells, and my brain continued to work overtime firing new thought-provoking questions and assumptions.

ASH

Samira tended to my injuries whilst I sat watching various members of the King's council pacing in front of me and chattering among themselves. Their brows furrowed in obvious distaste for the events that had unfolded, not that they would ever admit that to me.

'Care to share your discussions with your new king?'

I asked across the room. They immediately stopped, and their brows rose, a couple of mouths dropped open and flapped like hungry fish as they tried to work out how to respond.

'It wasn't a trick question.'

I was already bored of the mindless idiots who couldn't seem to process a world without my father leading them.

'I'm sorry Sire, we were just discussing... the funeral'

Glenn's eyes raced left and right as he very obviously tried to find something to say that didn't sound as offensive as the truth. I had to give credit where it was due, that was a good choice. His colleagues appeared to agree as they all nervously smiled falsely and nodded their heads too quickly to be believable.

'Excellent, you can arrange that I presume?'

I asked, intrigued to see their reaction. They were clearly shocked, but after a few seconds of glancing at each other, they nodded in unison. It was tradition for the new King to organise a respectful and extravagant funeral for the previous ruler. I had no interest in doing this.

'Yes sire, of course. Would you like us to run the proceedings past you before they are finalised?' Glenn twiddled his fingers awkwardly, clearly hopeful.

'Sure.'

I resigned myself to accepting that these simple creatures required a bit more of a structure and firm hand to function. They all sighed a breath of relief.

'Oh and we have already organised the removal of the Seelie guard from the premises sire, he has been sent back to his own realm. It would not do you any favours to be seen to be accommodating him here.'

I was about to argue their decision when the door to the room swung open and Ruby came into view. Her hair looked dishevelled and slightly matted, with dried blood sticking it together by the looks of it. Dirt and blood had painted her skin. But, she was still the most beautiful creature I had ever laid eyes upon. My heart swelled, as it had grown used to doing when she was near.

'Out.'

'Sorry sire?'

Glenn questioned.

'I said out, everyone get out.'

I did not dare tear my gaze from her for even a second. Ruby was safe and she was back with me where she belonged. When I didn't sense movement I put more force into my words.

'NOW!'

With this, they all scuttled away, including Samira who had dropped her swabs and ran. Ruby's eyes met mine and the pull between us was like magnets. The cool feeling of my magic hummed to life inside me as it awoke to meet hers. I pushed myself out of the seat and she ran towards me. Somehow we met relatively in the middle, and she threw her arms around my waist as she pressed her head to my chest

'I thought you were dead.'

I could hear her voice shake as she sobbed.

'For a minute out there I thought I was too.'

I laughed without any real humour. For a few minutes, I just held her, feeling her body tremble as she sobbed, until she finally ceased. I could feel Aoife and Saffie's uncomfortable presence, but could not bring myself to acknowledge them. My moment of being reunited with Ruby was all that mattered, to know that she was safe at last. Once she pulled away, she took my hands so that our contact remained.

'I think we will go and get Saffie back into the hospital bed she was so rudely plucked from.'

Aoife eventually offered, and then they both scurried out of the door. Ruby gazed after them for a moment, presumably questioning whether she should be following them. I gave a small, gentle tug on her hand to encourage her to face me again. I wasn't ready to let go of her just yet.

'So you're a King now.'

She remarked awkwardly before her eyes went wide and she looked worried.

'Oh no, I'm so sorry that was unbelievably insensitive of me. Aoife told me what you had to do, I am so sorry I can't even begin to imagine how you must feel.'

Her purity and innocence towards such things was something that I had surprisingly come to love. Previously I had seen it as irritating and all too human, however now I saw it as genuine kindness and that was an attribute that I now realised was lacking in my life until I met Ruby.

'You don't need to worry, it was the best possible outcome in that situation.'

I dared to stroke the side of her face and to my relief she leaned into the gesture, accepting my affection. Our magic twisted together and I could feel the warmth of her fire magic enveloping me gently. Without another thought, I leaned in and pressed my lips to hers. They were softer than I had imagined. She responded in turn and I felt her arms wrap around my neck. Flames licked instantly over my skin, but it didn't burn. Instead, it made me feel alive. My senses sparked as her intoxicating smell flooded me. The explosion of our magic truly connecting in that moment was overwhelming but incredible, more than I could ever have imagined it being. Ruby groaned as she experienced my ice magic sweeping over her. Two types of magic that should never have come together. Two Fae that should have never come together either.

Breaking apart, I had a realisation that there was no way I was ever willing to be separated from her. She was mine now and I was hers.

'Marry me.'

The words came out before I had even truly thought them through, but they made sense. By becoming queen, no one would question her motives again and we would be bound legally as well as spiritually. It was the only thing that made sense. Though, her hesitation made my heart beat a little faster and I found myself feeling anxious.

'Marry you? As in, become your wife and Queen?'

'That is correct'

'Can we do that?'

'I am King, we can if I say we can.'

I hadn't meant for it to elicit a laugh from her, but I was grateful to hear it. She remained pensive for another minute or so, though it felt a lot longer.

'Then yes!'

I felt elated at her acceptance of my proposal. The emotions I had been experiencing since meeting her were something I could never repay her for.

'What happens now though? There is still my supposedly mad brother on the loose.'

Her eyes were wide with expectation of me, an expectation that I would have answers and solutions. This was not something I had... but I couldn't let her know that. She needed words of comfort and security from me.

'Now, we get you cleaned up.'

I said as I teased a leaf from one of the matts in her hair.

'You look like you've been dragged through a forest by your feet.'

'You think you look any better?'

She laughed briefly.

EPILOGUE

ONE MONTH LATER

RUBY

I stared into the mirror, unable to take in or believe what I saw. A delicate chain of beautiful white flowers framed my crown and my long hair draped curls over my shoulders. A gorgeous white dress clung to my body in all of the right places, giving me a figure I was not even aware I had. White lace covered the bodice of the dress and extended into long sleeves. I half-turned in both directions many times, just admiring myself. I had never expected to be standing in a white dress on my own wedding day, especially not in a Fae realm betrothed to a Fae King. But here I was. There had been so many discussions on the practicality of it all. Whilst I understood Ash's argument about my new duties to the realm, as Queen, he was not as easy to explain my needs to. I was accepting of my new role and the adjustments that I would need to make to accommodate it, but I also was firm in my requests for access to the human world. I had friends there, friends that I would not abandon. Despite his discomfort and concerns, we were able to come to an agreement. I put my beloved home in the human world up for rent, as I couldn't bear the thought of selling it. I contacted Rob to let him know that I was okay and thanked him for the wonderful years working at his restaurant. It was the least I could do, and I felt guilty about that. As for my friends, they were informed that Ash and I had eloped, and we were organising a wedding reception party for when we returned from our travels. This meant that we would have chance to settle into our new roles a bit more before I dragged him back to my other world. Ash also conceded and agreed to attend any, and all, events in the human world that I wished to drag him to.

You look absolutely beautiful.

Saffie purred, a twinkle lighting her eye with emotion.

'Don't you dare cry Saff, I will not have mascara streaks on my wedding day.'

I grinned into the mirror at her.

You're about to be queen of the Unseelie realm, I think you have more worries than mascara streaks.

'Not today Saff, not today! Today I am focusing on that which I can control. Today, I can control not tripping on my gown as I go down the aisle, and making sure that I say the right words at the right time.'

I frowned at myself in a determined way and made an internal promise to allow myself the chance to just enjoy the moment. Over the last month I had struggled to come to terms with the rollercoaster of events that had occurred. I had thrown myself into learning my soon-to-be royal duties, and in my spare time, I worked on tracking down any potential leads for finding my brother. All of my efforts had come up fruitless. I had made myself exhausted and sick with determination to find him before he found us, the idea of him bringing about any further destruction was just unbearable. Two nights ago Ash had found me curled up among the books in the library, crying and throwing tantrum fireballs at books that did not provide me with any answers. He had scooped me up and carried me back to our room, ignoring my shouts and thrashing in his arms. That night he had stroked my hair and allowed me to scream, cry and just generally have a complete meltdown. I couldn't say how long it lasted, but it went on until there were no tears left, my voice was hoarse, and I lost myself to the unconscious.

'Thank you for everything you both have done for today.'

I turned and smiled warmly at both Saffie and Aoife who were watching my every move with a mixture of excitement and worry. Aoife stroked her growing belly absent-mindedly. I imagined that the wedding planning had helped her to focus on something other than her temporary 'desk-duty' restrictions. Saffie had been beside herself during my slight spiral of late, she had been at my side every minute that she could, allowing me her unwavering support despite her fear. In the slim spaces where she wasn't chaperoning my mental decline, she and Aoife had been planning my wedding for me. I hadn't quite expected the whole marriage thing to be quite so quick, and I certainly hadn't been in the right head space to even think much about it full stop. It had been established that Ash and I would need to 'unify' as they called it, though he assured me it was like a human marriage essentially, in order to solidify my role as queen and improve my protection. To be honest, I was fully okay with welcoming the opportunity to gain any sort of protection , and I certainly was not against speeding up linking my future with Ash. I had no idea what to expect of

Saffie and Aoife's wedding planning, but they had definitely nailed the dress and headpiece, so my confidence had grown in them since that reveal. With full optimism, I followed them both out of the room and towards my future.

'Ready?'

Aofie beamed at me, as we stood at the door that led out to the castle gardens.

'Definitely.'

This was quite possibly the only thing that I had been certain of in the last few months. Despite everything that had gone on, my and Ash's bond had only grown stronger, and my own control over my powers had grown with it. It was as though his magic helped to calm and mature mine. He had helped me to learn more about my magic and my abilities had even shocked him.

Aoife opened the door dramatically, and with an ear-to-ear grin. My jaw dropped and I felt the immediate moisture forming in my eyes which I did my best to bite back. The image ahead was an array of stunning white and red flowers paving the way down an aisle that ended with my breath-takingly handsome husband to be. His crisp black suit that he had very obviously picked to adhere to my human traditions was fitted perfectly to show off his slim but muscular frame. Guests were lined on either side of the aisle, all had turned to watch me. There had been times earlier in the month when hushed comments and snide remarks had been made about me, and they affected me right up until I had lost my temper. It turned out that losing my temper could lead to setting rooms on fire. Thankfully no one was hurt, but that certainly did stop the questions over my uselessness as a 'half breed'. That term was eradicated from people's vocabulary. I imagine it did invoke some level of fear, partic-ularly with my mother's history as queen. But that was an issue that would take time to address. I would prove myself worthy and fair.

If you were planning to run, it's too late.

Saffie mocked next to me as my feet failed to move. Chuckling back I mentally shook myself and stepped forward. He looked my way then, and our eyes met. So much emotion passed between us and a strong charge ignited between us as our magic reconnected. I had to urge myself to slow down then, and walk at a reasonable pace rather than run to him. The ceremony was an interesting mixture of Fae necessities and human additions for my benefit. Overall, it was absolutely incredible. Tears had flowed as soon as Ash had started speaking, and I couldn't tell at what point they stopped. Magic bursts of light had signalled the end of the official ceremony and seemed to replace the human confetti tradition. The after-party was as I had expected it to be, Fae wine and lots of it. Beautiful live music played throughout the rest of the day and into the evening, and I even managed to convince Ash to dance with me for a while, before Aoife became a more long-term dance partner for my evening. By the end of the evening, I had become very merry on Fae wine, as despite being careful my human side was still significantly more susceptible to its effects in comparison with those around me. I wrapped my arms around Ash's neck and kissed his cheek.

'Are we ready to go to bed now?'

I whispered into his ear. A grin spread across his face and he scooped me up into his arms in one quick sweeping motion. I squealed with excitement, and my friends cheered us goodnight as we made our way back into the castle.

He gently laid me down on to the bed and lifted my feet one by one to undo the straps of my heels and remove them. It was a constant amazement to me how he could be so gentle and sensitive with me and yet no one else had ever or would ever witness this side of him. It had been beaten down for so many years, and now he openly admitted to me that I was the only one he felt safe to show it to. The love I felt for him was indescribable and so pure.

'I love you.'

The words came out naturally without me thinking about them. He looked up then, and that amazing smile spread across his lips again.

'I love you too, forever.'

He crawled up the bed and lay beside me. His fingers stroked down my hair and tickled lightly down my arm until his fingers entwined with mine.

'I hope today was everything you had hoped for.'

His voice was gentle, but I could sense the slight concern behind it.

'It exceeded anything I could have even imagined. The word perfect doesn't even do it justice.'

I squeezed his hand gently in support.

'I know things have been hard for you lately. But, I want you to know that I will be there supporting you every step. We will find your brother, together.'

Just as his lips pressed to mine our door was flung open, Aoife and Bran ran breathlessly into the room.

'Privacy on our wedding night too much to ask for?!'

'It's Saffie! He's taken her!'

Aoife wheezed before dropping to the floor.

THE END

AFTERWORD

Thank you for taking the time to read Fae Bloodlines! I hope you have loved reading about Ruby's adventure so far, as much as I have loved writing it. If you would like to leave a review then I would be grateful for all feedback. For updates on book two, and further information on the Fae world described in the book please visit my website at:

www.jessicaboldauthor.co.uk